The Masks We Wear

A Short Sapphic Secret Identity Romance

Claerie Kavanaugh

The Masks We Wear

For information contact:

Claerie Kavanaugh

Email: claeriekauthor@gmail.com

http://www.halfcaffpress.com

First Edition: June 2025

10 9 8 7 6 5 4 3 2 1

Contents

Chapter One

♥

CHLOE

I slip sideways between two camera operators, ducking the bright overhead spotlights that make my teeth ache. My father's fundraiser surges with the kind of forced energy that exhausts me. Laughter that's a little too high, applause that's a little too quick. These people work for him or want something from him, so every angle is about image, leverage, or praise. My job? Stand near the podium, smile politely, and keep the doubts locked inside.

A staffer named Mallory hovers by the refreshment table. She notices my white-knuckled grip on the edge of a linen-draped slab of wood that's supposed to pass as a bar. "Everything okay, Ms. Scott?" She lifts a tray of sparkling water as if that might cure stale air and suffocating expectations.

I manage a tight nod. "Needed a breath. Where'd you put my father's coat?" It's a distraction question. I can't even hear her answer through the ringing in my ears. The scotch fumes, the cologne cloud, the swirling lights. My throat feels raw.

I force a laugh that tastes bitter on my tongue when Mallory tries to guide me to the safe corner she's arranged behind the stage curtains.

No. I can't spend another second reciting talking points. I pivot, scanning for an exit strategy. A glass door toward the back of the hall. That's my escape route. I slip into the hallway, ignoring the startled glance from a security guard who's used to seeing me comply. Not tonight. My heart slams in my chest like it wants out. The love seat near the stairwell reminds me of home—an inheritance of appearances that weigh a ton.

Then I see a ring of keys next to a campaign staffer's phone, left on a side table. My father's words echo in my head: "You're indispensable, Chloe." Meaning "Please don't cause trouble." But trouble is all I've got left if I don't escape. I snag the keys and keep moving.

Outside, the January night scrapes across my skin. I ignore the urgent beep of my phone buzzing in my coat pocket. The crisp air slices through the lacquered fundraiser vibe, and I inhale until my lungs shake. Snow dusts the sidewalk in front of the hotel. The hidden staff parking lot is almost empty. I find the staffer's compact sedan, beep the doors open, and slide in. My exhale fogs the windshield.

I drive. No plan. Just away. The Chicago skyline shrinks at my back, the big-shouldered city lights replaced by dark roads and fewer headlights. Each mile chips away at the tension in my neck. My father will call, Stevie will text, but I'm too tired to answer. Let them scramble. I need out.

Thirty minutes later, the roads narrow, and streetlights stand lonely in the hush of a small suburb. Fairford, the sign says. I downshift too hard, my pulse still fluttering from that breakaway. Any second guilt might roll over me, but right now I just keep going. Ahead, neon lettering burns bright against the cold: THE GETAWAY. My lips twitch in a half-grin I never show at home. Perfect.

I kill the engine and step onto the slushy pavement. Through the wide windows, I see a warm glow, a row of high stools, and a softly lit vintage jukebox. One push on the door, and I'm hit with scents of polished oak, beer hops, maybe a trace of something sweet like pu-erh. It's a welcome that feels different than the stiff corners of city events.

A woman behind the bar glances up. She's lean and tall, with tattooed arms and cropped dark hair that looks like it defies every attempt at styling. There's a skepticism in her eyes, but it doesn't feel unkind. She takes me in, from my wet shoes to my tailored blazer, then sets down the glass she's polishing.

"You good?" she asks in a low voice. No introduction, no pompous how-do-you-do.

I swallow hard. "I...do you serve tea?"

She snorts softly, caught between a grin and a shrug. "Not officially." She motions under the counter. "But I might have something kicking around."

I take a stool, my entire body thrumming with leftover adrenaline. "That would be amazing, thanks."

She stills, looking me over once more, as though most people who wander in here at this hour want whiskey, not tea. But she doesn't push. Instead, she pulls a tin from some hidden drawer, measures out a pinch into a small strainer, pours hot water from a kettle that definitely isn't standard bar stock.

Moments later, she slides it across the oak. The steam curls toward my face. My hands shake, and I wrap them tight around the mug, letting its heat seep into my fingers.

I try a sip. Subtle pu-erh, a little honey maybe. My shoulders drop an inch.

She leans against the back counter, arms folded, scanning me like I'm a puzzle. I can practically feel her question: what's your story? But she doesn't ask. In the hush of the bar, a track from the vintage jukebox starts up, some classic Springsteen tune about broken hearts and open highways.

I let out a wry chuckle. She quirks an eyebrow. "Funny?"

"Fits the mood." I hesitate, debating how much to say. "I saw the sign. 'The Getaway.' Seemed like as good a place as any for a pitstop."

She huffs a brief laugh. "You definitely don't look local."

I glance at my reflection in the mirror behind the row of liquor bottles. Makeup still set from the fundraiser, hair pinned in a style carefully tested for father-approved appearances. "Haven't felt local anywhere for a while."

She gives a slow nod. "Welcome to Fairford," she finally says. Then she turns to refill a beer for a bearded man at the corner, shoots me another measuring look, and leaves me to my tea.

Eventually, the door opens for a short burst—someone collects takeout, a couple orders a late-night drink—but mostly, it's me and this guarded bartender. She flicks her gaze my way, checks that the tea hasn't gone cold, but never volunteers small talk. And for reasons I can't articulate, that's perfect. I hate prying questions. I've built my life on deflecting them.

When my phone vibrates for the tenth time, I power it down. I can't deal with my father tonight. An odd swirl of guilt and triumph tangles in my chest. I blow on my tea, close my eyes, and let the tension seep out.

At closing time, the bartender—LOU, I notice on her stitched patch—collects used glasses. The overhead lights flicker a bit brighter, signaling last call. I fish a ten-dollar bill out of my coat pocket and slip it under the mug. It's more than the tea is worth, but I don't wait for change.

She picks up my empty cup, meeting my gaze for a pause. Her lashes lower as if she wants to say something but decides not to.

"Thank you," I whisper. "For..." I can't finish. I'm not sure what I'm thanking her for. A quiet place? A kind moment?

She just nods. "Drive safe."

My eyes burn. The simplest words carry a weight I can't explain. I manage a faint smile, then push out into the cold. The Getaway's neon sign glows above me, painting the snow in red and blue. As I walk to the borrowed car, I wonder if I'll ever return.

My breath clouds the air. I grip the door handle and slip inside. The tea's warmth lingers in my chest, the memory of her unreadable expression pinned under my ribs. I drive away, knowing there will be an onslaught of calls waiting. But right now, for one tiny moment, I'm free.

Chapter Two

Lou

I clock the headlights fading down Main Street, the faint swirl of exhaust fading into the dark. She's gone, although a piece of me is stuck on that trembling sigh when she touched the mug. Why do I care? I rub the tension from my forehead. Might just be that I recognize the look of someone running from a life they didn't ask for.

I collect stray coasters, wipe the bar, and keep catching myself glancing at the door like she's about to burst back in. Her tailored coat, her polished nails—definitely not from around here. She wasn't chatty, but her eyes had that caged-bird flicker. I've seen it before. I am it, sometimes.

The old jukebox stutters to the end of Springsteen, leaving the bar quiet enough for me to hear my own pulse. Tuesday nights usually crawl around here, so I shouldn't act surprised that only a handful of regulars trickled in. Yet this place was the busiest it's felt in weeks, just because of one worn-out woman with shaky hands.

By the time I tug down the metal shutters, I'm thinking about Thelma—my mother—and that last time she promised me we'd ride off into the horizon. Instead, she left me with credit-card fraud in my name and a busted teenage heart. After that, I learned not to count on people. They vanish. Even so, it's my business to serve the restless, the broken, the dreamers. And I like to think The Getaway is a place people can run to instead of running away.

I flip off the lights, leaving the neon sign flickering outside. The LED hum is my lullaby most nights. I snag my jacket from the hook by the door. My breath fogs as I cross the threshold into the bitter cold. I can almost hear Thelma's voice in my head. "Soon as you can, Lou, you get your own T-bird and drive out of these nowhere roads." She never gave me the chance. Or maybe I never took it.

I slip into my truck. It starts on the first try, which is a small miracle. The drive back to my studio apartment is short, just a few blocks away. After I park, I notice the passenger seat is covered in receipts, an empty coffee cup, and a half-read book about cross-country road trips. All these years, and I still haven't gone. I climb the creaky stairs to my unit above the hardware store, my joints protesting the winter chill.

Inside, I set my keys on the kitchen counter and pull off my boots. The faint hum of the overhead light does nothing to warm the emptiness. Tomorrow, I'll open the bar by noon and pretend not to wait for a certain stranger to wander in again, but maybe she will. Or maybe she's halfway back home by now, returning to whatever put that panicked look in her eyes.

My phone buzzes with a text. Probably from Bobby, my part-time bartender, checking the schedule. Instead, it's an unknown number. Could be spam. A jolt of anxiety nails me anyway. I check it.

Nothing. Blank screen. No message, just a glitch. I toss the phone on the small kitchen table, rummage for leftover pizza in the fridge. While I chew, my eyes wander to the single photo pinned on the corner of my mirror—the only decent picture I have of Thelma and me, back when life seemed full of possibility. I was ten, face freckled from the sun, arms around her waist like I feared she might disappear. Turns out I was right.

Sleep creeps up on me, but rest is rarely simple these days. I brush my teeth, yank off my clothes, drop onto the sagging couch that doubles as my bed. Memories swirl: the stranger's trembling hands, the heartbreak in her gaze. No name except the partial clue embroidered on her coat's lapel—C. Scott or something. Didn't matter. I'm not usually someone who obsesses about a random visitor.

But the sound of her voice clings to me. Like one more question might've broken her. I close my eyes. I need to forget. Sometimes I'm too good at forgetting—but tonight, my mind refuses to let her go.

Morning light slices across my face. I left the blinds partly open. Damn it. I tumble off the couch, elbow cracking against the side table. That's what I get for half-sleep in my jeans. The clock reads 8:15. Way too early for a bartender, but The Getaway won't open itself.

I drag myself to the shower, letting hot water pound between my shoulder blades. My thoughts land on the fact that I actually made tea for a customer last night. I never make tea. My regulars would laugh if they knew I kept a stash of pu-erh in a hidden drawer. But it's a small comfort on nights my own anxieties spike. If mothering myself is weird, fine—I'll do what I need to do.

Towel around my waist, I shuffle to the closet. I throw on a black T-shirt, worn denim, and my battered boots. I rummage in the drawer for that spare cologne bottle, the one with the scent that reminds me of weathered wood and open roads. As I swipe it on, I glimpse my reflection: short dark hair that sticks up in defiance, faint circles under hazel eyes. My lips press into a line. The day's young, and I'm already tired.

Downstairs, the hardware store's sign flickers OPEN. I push outside, giving a quick wave to Mrs. Greer behind the register. She pretends not to notice me leaving trash in the store's dumpster. Another perk of living upstairs. Then I cross the street to the bar, twist the front door lock, and step inside.

The bar is still asleep in that pre-opening hush. I toss my keys on the counter, flick on the lights, and head behind the bar to get the day's stock sorted. The glass racks need polishing, the beer lines need checking, and the surfaces require a quick wipe. I slip the hidden teabox out of its drawer to confirm the supply. Only a few bags left.

My chest tightens with a ridiculous surge of disappointment. If she comes back, I should be prepared. Then I catch myself. "Relax, Lou," I mutter. "People don't just come back. Not in your experience."

But minutes crawl by, and I can't stop glancing at the door. It's only midmorning. The regulars won't appear until later. A few lunch patrons might trickle in. Tourists on weekend days. Rarely do we get a fancy type unless they got lost. Maybe that's all it was: She got lost.

I organize the barstools, check the chalkboard sign for daily specials, and roll my shoulders to ease the tension. Then I move to my tiny office in the back, perched behind a battered metal desk. The computer runs slow, so I scroll invoices, check the numbers. My budget laughs at the idea of big expansions or new decor. This place is stable, but only just. Enough to live. Enough to keep me anchored in Fairford, even if I once swore I'd outrun it.

My gaze drifts to the borderline kitschy sign I've pinned on the wall: "Sometimes the only getaway you need is right where you are." One of those tacky truisms someone gave me as a bar-warming gift. I snort. More like a trap than a getaway. But it's mine, and I protect it.

Footsteps in the front. I push up from the desk, heart leaping. An early customer? The door creaks. In the bar area, a local plumber waves for a quick coffee to go. I fix it, charge a buck, make small talk about the weather. He leaves, and the door closes with a hollow click. The tension in my gut won't quit.

It's stupid to fret. She was just a stranger in trouble, not a friend. But the memory of how she inhaled that tea, like it saved her, keeps looping in my head. She had a question in her eyes, but no words to go with it.

I sink onto a stool, drumming my fingers on the polished oak. The jukebox rests silent for now, waiting for a coin. My phone vibrates in my pocket. I glance at the screen: unknown number. Probably spam again.

I set the phone aside, ignoring the swirl in my stomach. The day stretches ahead, ordinary as always. But it doesn't feel quite as ordinary anymore.

So I wait, telling myself I'm not waiting. Telling myself I don't care if she ever sets foot in here again. All my life, I've had one rule: Don't get attached to strangers. They'll leave. And you'll be the one reminding yourself that permanence is a fairy tale, as your mother taught you so well.

Still, I refill the hidden pu-erh canister just in case.

Chapter Three

Chloe

I'm gripping the steering wheel so tight my palms sting. One more slow exhale, one more pep talk. Doesn't help. The Getaway's neon sign flickers across my windshield, painting pinkish shadows on the dashboard. A week since my last mad dash here, and I'm still not sure why I can't stay away.

My phone buzzes in the cup holder. No way I'm answering that. Probably Stevie asking if I've reconsidered Dad's next media push. Possibly Dad himself demanding I decode some policy statement. Instead, I kill the engine and rest my forehead against the steering wheel. I mutter a few half-baked lines about being a freelance consultant, about preferring small-town ambiance for "research." A lie I've rehearsed to deflect suspicion if needed. But I only want to see Louise. Or Lou, or whatever she calls herself.

Finally, I swing open the car door and step onto the snowy pavement. My pulse hammers as I cross the threshold into the bar. Warm air hits first—then the soft overhead lights, reflecting off the polished oak. Tonight, three guys watch a sports channel on the far TV, but all I see is Lou behind the bar.

Her eyes flick up. There's a change in them—brief, flickering warmth. "Evening," she says, voice neutral except for the hint of a smile.

"Hey," I manage. My bravado shrinks to a whisper the minute she looks at me.

She sets aside the glass she's drying. "Tea again?"

For some reason, that tiny smile tugs at the corners of my mouth. "If it's not too much trouble."

Her smirk. "You're the only customer making me rummage through that stash. Gonna have to start charging a tea tax."

"I'd pay extra. Whatever you want." It escapes before I can filter it. My cheeks burn, and I clear my throat. "I mean—I appreciate it."

She just nods. Lowers her gaze. Turns to the hidden drawer and scoops out the pu-erh. The kettle's already humming, so it looks like she's started anticipating me. That thought warms me more than the overhead heat lamps.

I settle on the same stool as last time, peeling off my gloves. My coat? I keep it on for now, even though I'm toasty. Feels safer, like partial armor.

She sets the steaming mug in front of me. "So, Policy Consultant...work keeping you busy?" There's a teasing note, but also curiosity.

I swallow hard. "Busy enough. My clients prefer big-city politics, but I like to...take breaks."

Lou's brow quirks. "Fancy kind of break, coming all the way out here."

I glance around, avoiding her eyes. "You'd be surprised how refreshing it is." I take a sip, letting the floral taste settle my nerves. "I can breathe here."

She leans in slightly, crossing her tattooed arms on the bar. Her voice drops. "Glad to hear it, Tea Girl."

That nickname flips my stomach. "God, that must be the lamest bar handle you've doled out."

A low laugh rumbles from her chest. "Would you rather 'pu-erh Connoisseur'?"

I groan. "Oh, that's worse."

She shakes her head, eyes sparking with amusement, then steps away to help a customer waving for a refill. I watch her move—smooth, efficient, never skipping a beat as she handles glasses, taps, conversation, nonchalant as ever. I skim the row of liquor bottles, pink neon dancing in the reflective surfaces, and something in my chest unwinds. Maybe it's the lack of scrutiny. In my father's world, eyes track your every gesture. But here, nobody pries.

When she returns, I muster courage to speak. "So, do you always do more than bartend? Like, pick the music or something? I noticed the jukebox was on last time."

She shrugs. "You saw me feeding it quarters?"

I grin. "The track was Springsteen. A classic, if a little on the nose."

Her lips twitch. "I'm partial to Bruce and Stevie Nicks. Maybe I'm old school?"

I trace the rim of my mug. "I like anything with grit. Something that says life's messy, but we keep driving anyway."

Lou's gaze lingers on my face, and her expression softens. "Sounds like you'd get along fine with Springsteen, then."

I pick at a chipped spot in my nail polish. After a long pause, I glance at her. "What else you like to do...besides run a bar?"

She flicks a quick look at the guys on the other side of the room, adjusting her stance, maybe checking that no one's eavesdropping. Then she shrugs. "Read, sometimes. I got a stack of old road-trip memoirs. They remind me there's more to see. Yet here I am, still in Fairford."

My heart lifts. "Road-trip memoirs. That's...cool. Any favorites?"

She cracks a small smile. "Kerouac's too dusty for me, but I'm a sucker for those under-the-radar authors who drive cross-country and write about greasy diners. Beats reading the daily headlines."

I laugh—really laugh—for the first time in ages. "I'd love that. My schedule hasn't allowed many spontaneous trips." Understatement of the century. My entire life is meticulously orchestrated.

I hold her gaze, letting that admission out. Her eyes flicker like she wants to ask more. But instead, she nods, tapping the bar lightly. "Well, if you ever want recommendations, let me know."

And there in that moment, I feel...normal. Like I'm just a woman in a bar, chatting about books, sipping tea. No father breathing down my neck, no media lens dissecting my every move. This is real in a way I can't explain.

Eventually, the bar starts to empty. I realize I should probably head back—my phone has buzzed half a dozen times. I fish out a crumpled bill to pay. Lou scowls at it, but I insist. "You gave me a fresh bag of tea."

She shakes her head, pocketing the tip anyway. "Safe drive."

I slide off the stool, letting the coat swish around me. My heart thuds in a slow, heavy rhythm. I can't find a casual goodbye, so I just give a half-smile. "See you."

She says nothing, but I feel her gaze all the way to the door. The hush follows me outside, snow crunching underfoot.

Back in the car, I rest my hands on the wheel. My phone lights up with missed calls from Stevie, cryptic texts from my father. The usual script beckons: "Where are you, Chloe? What about the next interview?," etc. Right now, I don't care.

All I can think about is the smell of oak and pu-erh, and the gentle rasp of Lou's voice. I drive off, the bar's neon sign fading in my rearview, and for the first time in forever, my chest expands without strain. Maybe next time, I'll just tell her my name. The thought both thrills and terrifies me.

Chapter Four

Lou

Same corner stool. Same subtle perfume. Same flutter I try to shrug off every time she walks in. Another Thursday. Then the next one. And the next. By now, Tea Girl, whose name I'm since learned is Chloe, slides onto that seat at nine sharp, like clockwork, all quiet elegance with a hesitant smile.

I play it cool. I don't ask questions. She volunteers bits of her life, enough that I know she's legit about policy. She'll mention new headlines or city budgets. Her vantage on the world is so different from mine, but I like hearing her talk. She lights up when I call half the city council "a bunch of blowhards." My lack of filter makes her lips twitch in that hidden grin I chase each week.

Fallout of my mother's desertion taught me not to trust easy closeness, so I keep the bar between us. But something shifts each time she's here. Her posture unwinds, her laugh grows easier, and my chest feels too tight if I stare too long at the way her eyes crinkle when she smiles.

Tonight is the third Thursday in a row since her last reappearance. She's wearing a dark-blue coat, hair pinned back, and I'm cursing myself for how I notice every detail. I keep my expression neutral. "Usual?"

She nods. "Thanks, Lou."

I pause, sucking in a breath at how much I love hearing my name fall from her lips. My pulse stumbles. I clear my throat and refocus on preparing her pu-erh. "Busy day out there?"

She sighs. "Understatement. Some senator just introduced a flashy infrastructure bill."

I root around for a clean mug. "Is that good for people or just good PR?"

"Bit of both. Might fix some roads, or might grab headlines. Who knows. Politicians love a big show." Her tone becomes clipped, then she stops. "Sorry. I'm sure that sounds snobby."

I slide the steaming cup to her, leaning on the bar. "Nah. Not snobby. More like a realist."

She blows on the tea and meets my gaze. Her eyes flick down to my forearms, where the ink glints under the overhead light. "What's that design?" She reaches a fingertip, not quite touching, as though she wants to trace the lines of my tattoos.

I shrug, trying to quell the jolt in my gut. "A Thunderbird. My mother's dream car." My voice falters. Should I say more? She's never pushed, but we're teetering close to memories I keep locked. Against my better instincts, I continue. "We were gonna run away in one when I was a kid—just me, her, and an open highway. She disappeared instead."

Chloe stills. "I'm sorry."

I force a laugh. Funny how an apology from someone who's done nothing wrong can hit so deep. "Ah, that was years back. But it's why I named this place The Getaway. I figure I'll claim the dream on my own terms."

She leans in, eyes shining with an empathy that rattles me. I can handle pity; I get that sometimes. But genuine understanding? That's different. Suddenly I can't breathe. I busy myself wiping down the bar.

Her voice is quiet. "You stuck around, built something solid. I admire that."

I press my lips together, choosing not to answer. Because if I open up, I might say too much—like how I'm still furious at Mom, or how sometimes I wonder if I should hop in a car and never return. Or how Chloe's quiet presence is the gentlest thing I've felt in years.

We chat through the night. She details policy proposals, and I call a particular senator "a preening jackass." She snorts into her tea, half covering her mouth. That delight on her face hits me like a shot of adrenaline. I fire off more snark, watching her poise crack into real laughter.

Around midnight, the bar traffic has thinned to one last bleary-eyed couple and a guy scrolling his phone in the corner. Chloe's phone vibrates on the bar, but she ignores it. We're discussing my new set of craft beers. I offer her a sample sniff, even though she rarely drinks. She shrugs, grinning as she lifts it to her nose. "Crisp, kind of fruity."

I chuckle. "Works better if you actually taste it."

She takes a small sip. Her nose wrinkles. "No thanks. Too hoppy."

A flash goes off. K I catch the glare of a phone camera from the tipsy patron across the room. Before I can call him out, he slides his phone into his pocket and stumbles toward the door. Chloe looks at me, brow furrowed. "What was that?"

I exhale slowly. "Dunno. Some people take pictures for social me-dia. 'Hey, look where I am tonight.'"

She hesitates, fingers going rigid around her mug. "Right." A faint worry line folds across her forehead. Then she shifts, snapping out of it. "Probably an Instagram thing."

I figure it's no big deal. Sometimes people photograph the bar. But she's definitely rattled, so I murmur, "No harm, I bet."

After a moment, her stance relaxes. She runs a fingertip along the condensation ring on the bar. "I...like it here, Lou. Not sure how to say that without sounding sappy."

The air between us thickens. I wrestle with an urge to place my hand atop hers. That's not something I do. I keep customers at arm's length, always. But Chloe's not just a customer. Even if she should be.

"I like that you like it." My voice is barely louder than the hum of the jukebox. Then I shoot her a lopsided grin. "So...any chance you'll try the '66 Thunderbird dream yourself one day? Go off-grid?"

Her eyes flick up. "Sometimes I think about it. But I'm...tethered. People count on me. Not sure I can just leave that all behind."

I nod. More than she realizes, I get it. The bar's my tether. A life I both resent and protect. We fall silent, letting the jukebox fill the space. Some old Stevie Nicks track. She hums along. Her voice is beautiful and melodic. It sends a pulse through my chest.

Soon it's past three a.m. I gesture around. "I should close soon."

She sighs, then looks down at her tea cup, like she's searching for another reason to stay. Then she pushes off the stool, gathering her coat. "Yeah." A breath. "See you next week?"

My heart trips. "Sure. If you want."

Her lips curve in a soft, thankful smile. "I do."

My throat feels thick as I watch her go. Even as she's halfway to the door, I catch a final glance over her shoulder. Our eyes lock. I wonder if she'll ever call me Lou when we're anywhere but this bar.

The door latch clicks, and she's gone, leaving me in a hush that feels emptier than usual. I shut down the lights, do the closing routine, and ignore the wild rush in my chest.

But as hard as I try not to care, I know in my gut I'm already in too deep.

Chapter Five

Lou

I'm drying the last rocks glass, trying not to stare at Chloe's mouth. She's perched on her usual stool, cheeks flushed from a round of banter we both pretended was just talk. I catch a hint of mischief in her eyes and wonder if she can hear my pulse pounding. In my ears, it's loud enough to fill the bar. It's past closing, but I haven't turned on the bright lights yet. Didn't even hint at last call.

She fiddles with the napkin, winding it between her manicured fingers. Her hair's half loose, a few stray pieces framing her face. Snow dusts the window outside, but all I feel is heat radiating between us.

I set the glass aside, reach under the bar, and grab the bottle of reposado. Two fingers' worth is staff tradition—my private ritual that closes a good night. Tonight feels like something else altogether, but I keep it casual. Sliding a glass across, I pour carefully.

She eyes the liquor. "That's the stuff you mentioned last Thursday?" Her voice wobbles just a little.

"Yeah. Smooth, with a smoky finish." I gesture at her to take a sip.

Chloe lifts the glass, brings it to her lips. Her hand trembles. She tries to hide it, but I notice everything about her. She sips, nose crinkling at first, then her eyes flutter closed.

Something in my chest tugs. This is more than two strangers sharing a drink. This is me letting her see the part of me I usually keep locked up. Too dangerous. Too vulnerable.

She sets the glass down. "Lou, can I—"

Her question stalls, words tangling in her throat. She swallows, eyes darting up to meet mine. "You're the only reason I can breathe lately." The admission rushes out on a shaky breath. "I walk in here, and I remember who I am. Everywhere else, it's like I'm stuck in a costume."

My heart stutters. The raw honesty in her tone splits me wide open. I rub a hand over the back of my neck, trying to ground myself. Yet the more I look at her, the more I need.

Before I can overthink it, I round the bar. My footsteps echo in the hush. She's on that stool, knees parted slightly, and I step into the space. My palms find the edge of the bar on either side of her thighs. Her breath hitches. Her gaze flicks from my mouth to my eyes. I swallow, leaning in enough to feel the warmth of her body. "Tell me if you want me to stop," I murmur.

Chloe's answer is a kiss. Soft at first, a tentative brush of her lips that dissolves every thought in my head. I respond with equal caution, letting her show me how deep she wants to go. But she tilts forward, mouth opening against mine with a need that sets my nerves on fire.

My hands slide to her waist, fingertips pressing the smooth fabric of her blouse. She tastes like tequila–the one liquor I've managed to turn her onto–and something sweet I can't define. Her arms come up, fingers threading into the back of my shirt, pulling me closer. The stool wobbles under her shifting weight, so I ease a hand behind her to steady us.

A rush of heat flares through my veins. I deepen the kiss, inhaling the quiet gasp she releases. My thigh presses between hers, meeting soft warmth where her skirt rides up. Another shaky breath, then a burst of urgency. She fists my collar, tugging me closer until my chest touches hers, skin against skin where she's unbuttoned the top of her blouse.

My brain spins. I've wanted this so long—longer than I'd admit to anyone, including myself. She moans softly, tilting her head to give me more access. I shift my stance, pressing my body against hers. Tequila pulses through my blood, or maybe it's just her.

It's everything I swore I wouldn't do this fast. But her lips taste too good, her heartbeat thrumming against my palm. Her nails scrape lightly across my shoulder, finding bare skin under my shirt. I kiss the corner of her jaw, trail my mouth down her neck, feel the way her pulse flutters against my lips.

"God," she whispers, voice rough with want. "Lou..."

That one word cracks me wide open. My mind races with need, with longing, with a thousand half-buried fears. Because if we step off the ledge, if we let desire run wild, can we handle what comes after?

Her hand slides under my shirt. I arch toward her, mouth seeking hers again. She meets me in a heady swirl of tequila and pent-up longing. My lungs burn, but I can't stop. Then I feel that old voice in my head: don't rush or you'll wreck it. My mother's departure left me cautious to the point of self-sabotage.

I slow the kiss, pressing my forehead to hers. She's breathing hard, eyes glazed with want, and I can't believe how much I want to keep going. My entire body hums with it. But something inside me begs for control.

I ease my hands from her waist, still close but letting the moment breathe. My heart thunders so loud I can barely hear. "I'm sorry," I say, voice ragged.

Her eyes fly open, brow crinkling. "No. Don't apologize." She tries to kiss me again, lips gentle on my cheek, trailing to my mouth.

I let her for two beats that feel like a lifetime. Then I pull back, carefully pressing my hand to her shoulder. "It's not because I don't want to." My voice is raw. "I do. I really do." I drag in a shaky inhale. "But it's too fast. This is...important, right?"

She nods, eyes shining with understanding even though her face radiates heat and frustration. "Yeah. It is."

I brush my thumb along her lower lip, half wishing I could drag her behind the bar and never come up for air. But caution slams in again. If we're going to have something real, I don't want it overshadowed by fear or regrets.

Chloe takes a deep breath, smoothing her blouse. I catch a glimpse of flushed skin near her collar. She tries to fix her hair, lips pressed together in a wry smile.

"It's okay," she whispers. "I'm not going anywhere. Not if you don't want me to."

A warmth unfurls in my chest, chasing away the last echo of panic. I trace the edge of her sleeve. "I want you here. But I need time to figure out what that means."

She closes her eyes for a moment, like she's absorbing my words. Then she slides off the stool, her fingers still clinging to my shirt. I watch her gather her bag, her phone. Her cheeks are rosy, lips puffy from our kissing. She glances up at me with a promise flashing in her gaze.

"Next Thursday?" she asks, voice hushed.

A smile tugs at my mouth before I can hide it. "Like I'd miss that."

She exhales, relief coloring her features. Stepping away, she puts on her coat, buttoning it slowly. I stay rooted to the spot, arms crossed over my chest. It's taking every ounce of restraint not to pull her back into my arms. But I also know this is huge, and I don't want to blow it.

At the door, she glances back, a secret smile on her lips. I raise two fingers in a half wave. She slips outside, disappearing into the night that's cold and quiet except for the faint hum of The Getaway's neon sign.

The moment she's gone, I slump against the bar, heart still hammering. My arms feel the imprint of her, my skin tingling where she touched me. The bar is empty now, just me and the lingering taste of tequila on my tongue. I don't usually regret calling last call, but right now I'd trade just about anything for another hour of her.

I gather the glasses, tidy the bottles, anything to calm down. My reflection in the mirror behind the bar looks shattered with desire. I see the flush on my cheeks and let out a shaky laugh. All that talk about caution, yet I nearly pinned her to the stool. Another minute and I might've lost my head entirely.

But she didn't judge me for pulling away. She didn't beg or accuse. She just...understood. That's new in my world. Usually, people either push me too fast or vanish when I won't give them what they want. Chloe feels different. She leaves me thinking about next steps, next words, next touches.

I close up and do the final routine—lights off, floors swept. The hum of the fridge in the back storage sounds extra loud. Adrenaline still courses through me. I grab my jacket, locking the front door with unsteady hands. Outside, the cold wind hits my face, shocking me back into reality.

Halfway to my truck, I pause and tilt my head toward the sky, though the stars are faint behind town glare. My breath plumes in front of me, the night air still biting. I can't remember the last time I felt so uncertain and so alive.

As I start the engine, my mind replays the taste of her lips again. The way her breath caught when I touched her waist. The flash in her eyes when I said, "Tell me if you want me to stop." She had no intention of stopping. That knowledge coils in my belly, thrilling and terrifying.

I drive the deserted streets of Fairford, passing closed shops and the solitary stoplight. Everyone else is tucked in for the night, oblivious to the electricity that just sparked in my bar. My bar, which suddenly feels less like a lonely fortress.

At home, I climb the creaky steps to my apartment. Thelma's old photograph stares at me from the mirror. My teenage self clings to her waist, eyes full of naive hope. That memory used to burn, but something's shifting. Could be anger draining away. Could be that Chloe's presence changes how I see myself here.

I dump my keys on the coffee table, toe off my boots, and slump onto the couch. My mind spins with images of Chloe's parted lips, her small gasp when I pressed closer. I want so badly to pull her into my bed, bury my face in her neck. But I'm not rushing this. I won't risk turning what could be real into another fleeting affair that ends in regret.

Yawning, I let my head fall back against the couch cushions. The bar's quiet hum doesn't follow me here. Usually, I hate the silence, but tonight, it's a chance to sift through every detail of that almost-too-hot moment.

I smirk at how my heart still races. If I close my eyes, I can feel her nails on my back, her thigh shifting against mine. The pure need in her kiss. My entire body pulses with memory. But I also feel a strange sense of peace, like the vulnerability we shared might lead somewhere real.

Tomorrow, I'll probably second-guess letting her walk out as if I'm some aloof bartender playing it cool. But I'm not about to break a boundary we haven't fully set. She deserves more than a hurried fling behind a locked bar door. And, honestly, so do I.

I trace a circle on the couch fabric. I wonder if she's home safe. If she's replaying the same scene in her head. If she's wishing I hadn't stopped. If she wants me as badly as I want her. Then I realize I'm smiling like an idiot, and for once, I don't bother to stop.

Chapter Six

♥

Chloe

My phone flashes bright, like it's hurling news straight at my face. Everything else blurs. I'm on a stiff vinyl seat in Dad's campaign war room, half-eaten pastry growing stale on paper napkins, while a digital avalanche scrolls across my screen: WHO'S MELTING MAYOR SCOTT'S ICE-QUEEN? There I am, smirking in profile, leaning into Lou at the bar. The camera angle warps us into silhouettes more intimate than we actually were. But in politics, suggestion is enough to spark a match.

I cringe. Blood pounds in my ears. The item is trending, a hundred comments a minute. Too many mentions about me "rebelling" or "finally showing some emotion" or "clinging to a shady bartender." My father paces by the podium, face tight. Two staffers whisper behind thick binders. The overhead lights hum with bureaucratic tension.

He slams a folder onto the table. "I told you to keep your personal life under the radar," he says, voice low but lethal. "Optics, Chloe, always optics."

My heartbeat struggles under his glare. I remind myself to keep my spine elongated, just like etiquette lessons taught me. "I only stepped out for a quiet drink," I say. "There's no story."

His campaign manager, Janine, cuts in: "If there's a quiet drink with a woman, the tabloids call it scandal. We have to run damage control."

Dad exhales slowly. His eyes flick to the door, as if scanning for intruders. This office is all glass and metal edges—no place for a meltdown. "We'll handle it," he says. Then he turns, opens a small ivory box, and pulls out a common blue orchid brooch. "Pin this to your coat," he says. "Discreet panic button with a live security feed. We can track you, notify authorities if anything goes wrong." His words sound official, caring even, but I see the trap.

I swallow, nauseous. He lifts the brooch closer, turning it so I catch the reflection of the hidden lens in the opalescent surface. My father mistakes my hesitation for fear. "If you won't use it," he says, "I'll freeze funding for your children's literacy program and increase your security detail around the clock."

The bite in his voice leaves no debate. My face feels hot. "You'd hold that program hostage?"

He doesn't answer. He just sets the brooch on the table between us. I fold my arms over my stomach. My father stands, adjusts his cufflinks, and dismisses the staffers with a curt wave. The door clicks shut. Now it's just me, him, and the thunder of fluorescent lights overhead.

He steps closer. "Wear it whenever you visit that dive. We can't afford more surprises." A single white hair flutters at his temple as he delivers the ultimatum.

I think of Lou's look last night. The corners of her hazel eyes, the subtle warmth behind her sarcasm. The shaky grin when I teased her about chamomile tea. I want to be done with lying. But I'm too tangled.

I force my fingers to wrap around the brooch. "Fine," I say. "Now may I go?"

He nods stiffly. No I love you, no Are you okay? We part ways with unspoken hostility. As soon as I'm beyond the campaign doors, I duck into my car and toss the box onto the passenger seat. My mind pulses with a hundred retorts I didn't dare say out loud.

At the first red light, I stew. I should refuse to spy on Lou. Spy. That's exactly what this is. Are we so far gone that gentle, guarded Lou is some threat? My stomach lurches. Then reality hits: my father is never subtle. If I fight now, he'll shred the one project that matters most to me. He'll plaster security guards at my apartment, or worse.

At home, I drop my purse on the marble foyer, slip off my heels, and retreat to my bedroom closet. This closet is my only real hiding place—rows of color-coordinated suits and tastefully curated shoes can't talk back. I flick on the overhead light and sink against the mirrored door. Then I press the brooch's edges until I feel them crack. The device doesn't break, of course, but I can't stand the smoothness. My phone hums with Dad's aide sending "installation instructions," which I instantly delete.

Lou's flannel, the one she lent me when we parted ways a few nights ago, rests in a corner. I grab it. It still smells faintly of her cinnamon-oak cologne. I bury my face in the soft cotton and something breaks inside me. Hot tears spill down my cheeks. I clench my jaw to keep the sobs from echoing in the hallway.

A wave of guilt rises next. I haven't told Lou about the conditions. Any contact with me now means a hidden mic. My father might be listening. Is that who I am? The daughter of a megalomaniac mayor who's forcing my hand?

An hour must pass, maybe more. My phone keeps buzzing with notifications. Text from Stevie: "Damage control is in progress. Don't do anything rash." The next message from an unknown number: "Saw the article. Guess you're not so frosty after all. Good luck, Princess." I fling the phone aside. Old nightmares jostle for space in my head. My mother's face the day she left for "treatment." The headlines about her rumored affair. The hush-money deals. The quiet heartbreak that shredded my family.

I use Lou's flannel to wipe my cheeks. The plush cotton is damp now, but I won't let it go. I breathe in that faint cinnamon smell and force my trembling to still. I push off from the floor, yank the bedroom door open, and stride out, collecting myself.

I can't run from this. So I do the only thing I can. I tuck the common blue orchid brooch away in my purse, refusing to pin it anywhere. Let Dad think I'm obedient. Let him think I'm docile. His scrutiny won't stop me from seeing Lou. But guilt rattles me like a stray bullet. I just need to figure out how to explain, or if I dare explain at all.

For now, I stand by my bedroom window, phone in hand. My reflection looks small, eyes still puffy. I debate texting Lou. Telling her everything might burn me. Not telling her might kill us before we can even begin.

I'm so tired of living behind frosted glass.

Chapter Seven

Lou

I'm wiping down the counter at The Getaway, half-lulled by the spotlight from the neon sign. It's near midnight, the sweet hour when the real confessions sometimes spill. My phone's silent. Chloe hasn't called all day. But I can't stalk her feed or read any more headlines. I stand in my bar, polishing the same glass over and over, hoping she might walk through the door.

Then she does.

Chloe steps in, shoulders hunched. She's wearing a simple black coat, buttoned against the cold. No fancy pearls tonight. Her eyes dart across the empty tables. I set down the glass. She must read my expression because she lifts a hand in apology before I can speak.

"Can we go for a drive?" she asks, voice nearly lost in the hum of the jukebox. "I just...need space."

I grab my jacket without hesitation. Maybe I should ask a million questions about what's wrong, but the hollow sound in her voice crushes me. We leave The Getaway, locked up behind us, side by side in the dim streetlight.

Her car is sleek, city-smooth, not the battered pickup I might've expected. I slide into the driver's seat as she requests—my eyebrows rise, but I don't question it. She keeps her gaze on me, hands shaking.

I start the ignition. "Where to?"

She doesn't answer, just touches the back of my hand. "Anywhere not here."

I nod. We roll through empty streets, past dark storefronts and the vacant motel. The shape of small-town Fairford at midnight is lonely and comforting all at once. She doesn't talk. I don't push. The tension in her posture is obvious, though. Something is tearing at her.

Eventually, I steer us toward the deserted lakeside docks, where winter has half-frozen the water's surface. I park near a battered old sign. The moon glances off patches of ice beyond the rotted pier.

Chloe stares out the window. "I hate headlines," she whispers. "I hate them so much."

I kill the engine. The heater hum persists, swirling warmth around us. "You can stay here as long as you want," I say. "We don't need to talk about it." But that's a lie—I'm dying to know. Still, I wait.

She closes her eyes. "The stories are never accurate. They spin everything. Sometimes I feel like I'm just a brand."

I don't respond. Instead, I rest a hand gently against her shoulder. Her hair brushes my fingertips. She turns, eyes brimming with unshed tears.

She laughs, and it's a broken, shaky sound. "You don't even ask me for details."

"Figured I'd let you tell me if you want."

"But supposing you're part of the story," she says, voice catching. "What if people drag you into my mess?"

I muster a half-smile. "Wouldn't be the first time I got called 'shady barkeep.' I can handle it."

She exhales, tension leaving her shoulders. Then she looks around the car, as if searching for the right words. "I get panic flashes. Cameras, father, pressure. I see them in my sleep. Cold sweats. Everyone telling me what to do, who to be with, how to breathe." Her eyes lift to my face. "I came here to feel something real."

My throat closes. Her confession rings too close to my own locked-up fears. "For what it's worth," I say, "I haven't left Illinois since my mother split. That's my version of panic. Being stuck. Waiting for something to go wrong."

"Do you regret it?"

I frown. "Regret not chasing her? Or regret not chasing my own life?"

Chloe shifts in her seat, turning toward me. The overhead lamp highlights the dark circles under her eyes. "Both."

Instead of answering, I ask, "Do you regret coming here tonight?"

Her jaw clenches. "No. I regret not coming sooner."

We reach for each other almost at the same time. My seatbelt digs into my side as I lean across the console. She meets me halfway, breath warm against my cheek. A ripple of heat rushes through me. I cup her face; her lips part against mine in a quiet plea. She climbs across the console, pressing close. The gear shift jabs her hip, but she doesn't pull away.

Her hands grip the collar of my jacket. She's trembling. My pulse goes wild. I brush my thumb along her jaw, just enough to coax a soft sigh from her. She kisses me again, deeper this time. The windows fog up, moisture beading on the glass.

"Lou," she whispers, voice husky. She moves onto my lap, knees on either side of me. My heart hammers. The car smells like leather and her perfume, something faintly floral. Every nerve I have flips on like a switch.

I don't rush. My hands settle on her waist, feeling the subtle quake of her body. She exhales a quiet moan as I trail my lips to that soft spot beneath her ear. Our desire builds, heads hazy as I tug her coat aside. Warmth arcs between us.

Her phone suddenly buzzes. Or maybe it's something else. There's a faint vibration, a muffled hum. She tenses so hard I can practically feel her heart slam in her chest. "Wait," she mutters. She shifts, rummaging in her coat pocket until she pulls out a small, round common blue orchid brooch. The vibration skitters across my leg.

"That's your father calling?" I ask, confused.

She holds the brooch up like it's a poisonous spider. "He gave me this. Says it's a panic button." Her laugh is hollow. "He's calling through it."

The intimacy cracks wide open. I feel her pulling back, burying the moment under a fresh wave of fear. She flips the brooch facedown on the dash. The vibration stops. My breathing struggles to calm, but she swallows back a sob.

"I'm sorry," she says, voice ragged. "This is so messed up. I thought I could—" She closes her eyes. The admission dangles half-formed in the air.

I rub my thumb over her knuckles. "Chloe, you don't have to explain. You're in a tough spot."

She looks at me with raw regret. "I'm not okay."

I nod, chest tightened. She's not okay. Neither am I. Because that next kiss I wanted—that taste of proof that something good can last—just slipped away like water through fingers.

She straightens, climbs off my lap. The heater's hum feels invasive now. My arms suddenly feel cold. I wrestle with the seatbelt so she can move back into the passenger seat. Silence. Then her voice cracks: "Can you drive me home?"

I manage a short nod. No quips, no teasing sarcasm. My mind reels with the knowledge that her father is monitoring her. That I almost spilled all my personal truths into a hidden mic. I squeeze the steering wheel as she fastens her seatbelt. The closeness we shared is replaced by a charged emptiness.

We drive quietly along the lake road, the reflection of headlights dancing on patches of ice. She keeps the brooch flattened on the dash, not even glancing at it. I sense her shame and anger. I sense my own confusion swirling around us.

When I pull up to her building, she thanks me with watery eyes. I touch her hand—just once—before she slides out. No more kisses. No mention of tomorrow. She walks away, shoulders bowed, coat flapping in the wind.

I watch her disappear inside, the light swallowing her form.

I drive back to The Getaway, alone, body thrumming from a kiss that ended too soon. My mother used to talk about freedom, how it waited just beyond the next horizon.

Inside the bar, I switch on the overhead lights and toss my keys on the shelf. There's a hidden drawer by the sink with chamomile tea bags. Lately they've just been for Chloe, but tonight I rip one open for myself. The water runs scalding hot, steam clouding my reflection in the metal faucet.

I sip, each swallow calming the quake in my veins. Then I sink onto a barstool, phone in hand, wondering if I should text her. Check if she's okay. But I've learned not to push. I glance at the door, waiting for a sign she might come back—some crazy midnight miracle.

Nothing. Just me, the hum of the lights, and the ghost of her warmth across my thighs. She asked to feel something real. I felt it, too. Now I just need to believe this isn't the end.

I close my eyes, replaying the taste of her lips. The heartbreak and hope swirling together. Stuck. But for the first time in years, I want to believe in permanence. Even if it's just a flicker. Because the way she looked at me in that car—like I might be the safe place she's never had—that shines brighter than any neon sign.

I don't know how this ends. But I'm not walking away.

Chapter Eight

♥

Chloe

I'm in my car outside Lou's bar, engine idling, phone on silent. Only a handful of hours ago, Dad's office texted me for "updates." They want drama. Proof that I'm discreetly milking every rumor. I've ignored them all. The guilt clings to me like tar. Each time my phone lights up, I picture some staffer hoping I'll spill scandalous details. Every minute I spend lingering here, I wonder if I'm risking her trust.

I won't go inside. The brooch freaks me out. Switching it off worked once or twice, but the paranoia never stops. If the device picks up anything at The Getaway, Dad will wedge himself between us. So I won't let it happen. Instead, I text Lou from the parking lot: "Ice cream? I'm craving mint chocolate." She replies almost immediately: "On my way."

We end up at a garish neon parlor—the only ice-cream spot open this late. A bored teenager behind the counter watches us like we're the only source of entertainment all week. Lou and I fumble through plastic spoons. She tries to make me laugh, conjuring a smirk by guessing which ridiculous flavor I'll sample next. Bubblegum swirl? Peanut butter bacon? For a split second, I forget to be anxious. Then my phone buzzes with lagain, short requests demanding updates. I turn the phone facedown. Lou doesn't press. Instead, she taps the edge of my waffle cone. "Spill or don't—your choice."

She's too gentle for her own good. Some nights, the thought of betraying her inadvertently crushes me. I let the moment slide. We move on to an antique bookstore, then a closed planetarium whose staff I know from charity events. I talk us past security, which earns me an odd look from Lou. We step into the dome, guided only by the emergency lighting. I watch Lou inhale the hush of it all. Stars swirl overhead in projected illusions. The faint hum from the projectors draws me close to her. I want to hold her hand, soak in the comfort, but I can't let the brooch come anywhere near her. Better to keep my father's range worthless.

After an hour, Lou glances at her watch. "I've got an early shift tomorrow. Might need to bail. You want a ride home?"

I nod, pretending it's no big deal. The walk back to her car is heavy. Jazz music drifts from a bar down the street. She hesitates, probably itching to ask why I avoid The Getaway. I can't bring myself to explain the half-truth or the wires. So I rest my head on her shoulder, letting guilt twist my stomach. She drives me home in silence. Alone in my kitchen, I cradle my phone. How long can I deflect?

·

We keep this pattern going for days. Drive-thru coffee. Late-night donuts. We laugh momentarily, share stolen kisses in deserted parking lots. But the second she mentions returning to her bar, my chest constricts. I make excuses—"It's too crowded."

She nods. She never complains outright. Still, her face shadows whenever I steer us somewhere else.

She's missing shifts, losing tips. I know The Getaway is more than a job to her. It's her safe place. And here I am, urging her away to protect my secrets. More guilt. I catch glimpses of headlines about me being a "wildcard," about Dad's staff trying to salvage my image. I want to throw my phone in the river. At night, I replay conversations. I picture telling Lou everything: the bug, my father's threats, the funding for my literacy program. Each time, fear grips my throat. If she sees me as a liar, she'll walk.

Eventually, it's an another ordinary weeknight, no big extravagance. We're in her truck because her car refused to start. The radio hums with Stevie Nicks. We're parked near a quiet diner, sipping watery coffee. Her forearm rests on the wheel, showcasing the swirl of tattoos. The overhead light sputters. I notice how she scoots closer whenever someone passes like she's silently shielding me. I'm not sure from what, but the warmth soothes me.

Her phone pings with an alert from one of her employees: The Getaway is swamped, short-staffed again. A line forms outside. "We gotta go," she murmurs, sounding hesitant, "this is too many nights I'm ditching my place."

I trace a circle on my coffee cup. "I know."

She watches me. Then she says, "Chloe, is everything okay? I don't mind going out, but you seem...on edge."

My heart leaps into my throat. My hands tremble around the cardboard cup. "I just—there's a lot with my father. He doesn't like me at your bar."

Lou's expression clouds. "Figured that. But you can't keep running around the outskirts of town forever."

I set my coffee down so I don't spill. "Sometimes I wonder what life would be if I left Chicago's politics behind. Or if you left Fairford." I shoot her a sideways glance, desperate for reassurance that maybe endings aren't inevitable.

She wipes a spot on the steering wheel. "You asking if I'd quit everything?"

I shrug, forcing a half-smile. "Yeah. Ever dream of starting fresh? No baggage. Just something new."

She clenches her jaw. A world of pain banks behind those hazel eyes. "People like me don't get new beginnings," she says softly. "We patch what's left and call it home."

My stomach twists. I could blurt every hidden detail: the wire, the forced arrangement, the texts I'm hiding. But I'm paralyzed. Terrified. If I come clean, she might see me as no better than the people who used her before. I swallow back the confession, tasting salt. A tension-filled quiet stretches. When she finally drives us to The Getaway, her parting hug lingers with unspoken questions. I walk away feeling like I'm balancing on a fraying tightrope, each day riskier than the last.

•

The next day, we try a coffee shop near the outskirts, some cutesy place with crocheted seat covers. Lou's uneasy. The smell of vanilla beans saturates the air, but she drinks with forced politeness. Her phone vibrates again. I see fleeting disappointment in her eyes—someone else covering her shift last-minute. My gut churns. I'm costing her money. Security staff from Dad's office keep texting me: "Any bar intel?" I delete each message. They'll probably escalate soon, demand real evidence or threaten to sabotage my literacy program. My panic grows by the hour.

I stir my latte, not tasting the sugar at all. Lou is rambling about the broken jukebox at The Getaway, how she found a local electrician to fix it. Her tone is bright, but something in her posture is guarded. Like she's waiting for me to stop dancing around whatever's wrong. I imagine telling her, "It's me. My father gave me a mic and expects me to play spy." But I lock my lips.

I look at her hands, the faint scars, the swirling tattoos. The Thunderbird She deserves better than my half-lies. The sting of tears pricks my eyes. "I'm sorry," I blurt at last, though it barely scratches the surface.

She reaches to over squeeze my wrist. "For what?"

I choke on words I can't say. "For...all this running around."

Her eyes soften. "It's OK." She says it with enough conviction to make my heart skip. I try to believe those words. But the guilt is there, thick as smoke, reminding me we can't outrun the truth forever.

Chapter Nine

Lou

Thursday creeps up, and I notice she's gone quiet. No texts, no calls, nothing. My staff jokes that I've got the "lovesick jitters." They're not wrong. By late evening, the bar's half-full, but I'm too uneasy. Where is she?

I revolve through emotions: annoyance, worry, confusion. She's hidden some piece of her life, obviously. But I kept giving her space. Maybe that was a mistake. Around ten at night, a rowdy guy at the end of the bar yells for another round. I pour drinks, ignoring the flick in my gut that says something's off.

Then a regular, Chlyler, leans over the counter, eyes wide. "You seen this?" she asks, jabbing her phone at me. "Some blog posted about the mayor's daughter. Says she's playing informant at a local bar." She taps the screen, scrolling too fast for me to read. "Says the bar's an alleged love nest."

My stomach plunges. I snatch the phone, eyes flicking across the text: MAYOR'S DAUGHTER'S LOVE NEST TIED TO FOUNDATION LEAK?. The article claims she used hidden tech to gather inside info. They're naming The Getaway, hinting at me. Some watchers apparently suspect Chloe was wearing a device. That would mean she's passing political dirt to get favors. My chest burns. My memory flashes to headlines about my mother's credit-card scam, the lovers who ghosted me after prying into my finances. My heart slams in my chest.

Anger floods me. "Sorry, folks," I say. "Closing early tonight." There's confusion, grumbles. I pretend we've had an equipment malfunction. The bar empties. I lock the doors, flick off the neon sign, but the pink glow sputters in protest. I storm upstairs to the cramped office.

I slam the door behind me, breath ragged. My phone sits on the desk. No messages from Chloe. The many times she swore she was done letting other people control her.

But the article has an entire angle about how she's exchanging intel for hush money or an advantage in some political scheme.

I pace the tiny space, stepping over boxes of old receipts. My mother's face surfaces in my mind, bright with false promises. She left me with fraud debt that took years to pay off. Then every lover who showed up with sweet lines, only to vanish. The first time I saw Chloe, I sensed something different—an honesty behind her eyes. Was that a lie too?

My head pounds. I scroll through her socials. She's posted nothing all day.

The creeping silence feels like a sucker punch. C. Scott. Of course. I should have known. Her father's a politician. She was raised in a spin factory. She probably doesn't even see me as real. I brace my hands on the desk, old flyers for an open-mic night crinkling under my palms. My breath comes in shallow bursts. A swirl of memories hits me: the way she looked at me under that planetarium dome, the ease with which we kissed, the tremble in her voice. Was any of it honest?

I yank open a file cabinet, rummaging for something. I find a crumpled photograph of The Getaway's grand-opening day. I look young, hopeful. I believed I had total control.

Stupid.

My phone pings with a missed call from Bobby. I don't answer.

I jam the desk drawer shut, almost catching my fingers.

"Why'd you do this?"

The furious part of me wants to believe she's just another user, the next in line to exploit my trust. The part of me that yearns for her is crushed under the weight of betrayal.

Tossing my jacket on a chair, I sink onto the worn couch stuffed under the single window. My reflection in the glass looks older, cheeks hollow with fatigue. "You idiot," I mutter to myself. "You let her in." Now I'm paying the price. Outside, the neon sign flickers again, flick-flick-flick, mocking me with its pink glow. My phone vibrates. A text from an unknown number: "Better watch your back. The mayor's daughter sold you out." My throat constricts. fling the phone across the room. It clatters to the floor with a crack.

Anger tastes metallic on my tongue, but beneath it all, I'm devastated. Did she care at all? She came in night after night, asking me to drive, to hide away in corners of town, avoiding my bar like it's toxic. Was that the plan? Keep me close, gather my secrets, then vanish?

I snap the overhead lamp off, letting the dark swallow me. My mind replays the first time she walked into The Getaway, that hesitant half-smile, the way she set aside her expensive coat. Intelligent, cautious, haunted. Now, I guess, manipulative. A tear stings my eye, but I wipe it away so fiercely my skin burns.

I rummage the desk for a half-empty bottle of whiskey, ignoring how it stings my throat when I take a swig. Normally, I'd never do this. Tonight, I don't care. The warmth only fuels my anger. I slap the bottle down, snatch my phone, and consider texting her: "Don't ever come back." But my finger hovers over the Send button. I can't bring myself to do it. Maybe some pathetic piece of me hopes there's an explanation.

A memory flickers: the bruise-colored circles under her eyes when she told me she hates headlines. That moment in the truck when she said she was sorry without telling me why. Could this be some twisted spin job by the media? God knows they lie. But if she's not reaching out now, maybe she doesn't want to.

I flip the wall switch, flooding the cramped office with light. I have a business to run, staff to pay. As for her, I guess she's proved me right about letting people in. I tumble into the old desk chair. There's a dryness in my throat that whiskey doesn't quench.

Downstairs, the silence is deafening. No glassware clinks. No chatter. Just the flick-flick of the neon. I close my eyes, blocking out the memory of how her hand felt in mine. If she's out there collecting political scraps at my expense, that's it. She's gone.

I force myself to stand, gather receipts to distract my brain. But I can't focus on numbers. My jaw aches from grinding my teeth. The article's headline replays in my mind. I thought she was different but close Scott turned out to be exactly who I thought. A heartbreak I should've seen coming. I run a hand over my short hair, messing it further. Enough. Tomorrow, I'll open the bar and face the gossip. Then I'll move on—no illusions, no second chances.

If she wanted me to trust her, she should've stayed honest. Or said something. But she vanished instead. Now I'm left to pick up the piece. Again.

Part of me wants to leap into a car, track her down, force the truth out of her. But I know better. People can't be forced to care. They either stay, or they don't. She made her choice.

Sinking back against the desk, I stare at the flickering neon through the window. That sign used to symbolize escape. A safe haven for everyone who needed a second chance. The promise that maybe I needed saving, too, and thought I'd found it in her. Now it's nothing but the final punchline.

Chapter Ten

Chloe

I'm halfway through shaking hands at a charity brunch when my lungs begin to fail me. Cameras flash, the mayor's staffers watch me like hawks, and every inch of my skin feels like it's crawling with guilt. Two days since the story leaked. Two days without word from Lou. I plaster on a polite smile for the photographers, but their lenses seem to pierce straight through my facade.

Glittering silverware clinks across linen-draped tables. Warm chandeliers paint the walls in gold. One socialite waxes on about city improvements while another leans in, voice dropping conspiratorially, "Can you comment on the bar fiasco, dear?" I freeze, ears ringing. My father's staff insisted I attend this event, to show the public I'm still the pristine politician's daughter. I feel like a mannequin, propped up for display.

After dessert is served—some airy confection I can't taste—shadows dance at the edges of my vision. Too many bodies press close. Heat blooms under my collar. I excuse myself with a brittle laugh, muttering something about the restrooms. The corridor outside the banquet hall is dimmer, quiet, but the hush only amplifies my shaky breathing.

My stomach knots. I stumble until I find a service hallway. My knees buckle, and I slump against expensive silk wallpaper.

Air refuses to enter my lungs properly. Everything spins. There's a roaring in my ears, like a distant crowd. I cling to the wall, nails scraping the fancy fabric. Then a weight presses gently on my shoulder. Stevie. His expression is grim, all the usual slick confidence dimming under concern. He doesn't say a word at first, just fishes keys from his pocket.

He angles his body to shield me from any passing staff. "Bad shrimp," Stevie murmurs, as if rehearsing a lie. "That'll be our story to get you out of here." I manage a nod, gulping oxygen in ragged sips. He tucks me under his arm, guiding me to a side exit. Camera shutters echo in distant corridors, but we slip away.

Forty-five minutes later, we're parked outside The Getaway. The neon sign is on, but through the windows, I spot no movement, no sign of her. My fingers grip the iron railing until pain shoots through my palms. Stevie stands behind me, shuffling like he's debating some bold confession. When he finally speaks, his voice is uncharacteristically tender. "I never actually passed your intel to Dad," he says. "I wanted to keep him off your back so you had room to breathe."

My throat closes. The words soothe some part of me, but the bigger fracture stays raw. "He threatened everything I care about," I whisper. "I felt cornered." My voice cracks on the last syllable. I think of Lou's eyes, the moment I nearly told her about the brooch, how I ended up fleeing instead. The memory slices through me.

Stevie gently places a hand on my shoulder. "Kiddo, I'm sorry," he says. "I didn't realize how deep this would cut. If you need more time, more space, I can—"

He stops, noticing my tears. A biting January wind stings my cheeks. The silence between us is thick. Finally, he offers me the car keys again, gesturing toward a coffee place next door. "I'll grab us something hot. You decide if you want to go inside."

I glance toward the bar's door. My heart lurches at the thought of facing Lou, explaining my tangled lies. I can't do it, not while my pulse still feels like a trapped bird. So I remain there, my knuckles white on the railing, breath fogging in the cold. Maybe I'm a coward, but right now, I don't know how to cross that threshold.

Stevie steps away, guilt etched on his face. His footsteps fade, and I'm alone with the neon glow flickering across the pavement. I ache to see Lou, to explain why I went silent. But the fear of her rejection locks my feet in place. So I stand there, fighting tears. If I open that door and glimpse her expression, maybe I'll never recover. I need to steady myself before I lose everything. Maybe I already have.

Lou

Bobby corners me after closing and says, "Chloe came by. She stood outside for an hour, never once tried to come in." That image whipsaws my gut. I imagine her shivering under the neon. A hundred thoughts swirl: she must be afraid, or ashamed, or both. I swallow, trying to keep my expression neutral, but Bobby sees right through me.

"She's hurting," Bobby says. Then they unfold a newspaper op-ed, pushing it within reach. The bold letters read IS CHLOE SCOTT SACRIFICING HERSELF FOR OPTICS? By Stevie Scott. I skim it, stomach clenched. He's speculating Chloe might publicly break from her father's political machine, painting her as a pawn who's ready to implode her own narrative. My anger softens into a frightened ache. If she's about to go nuclear on her father, that means she'll face tidal waves of scrutiny.

I toss the op-ed on the bar and exhale. Bobby squeezes my shoulder. "Maybe you should talk to her, boss," they say quietly. Their words jab at the guilt I've been nursing. For two days, I've stewed in bitterness. Now I don't know how to untangle the facts. Did she really spy on me, or is this all twisted rumor? The memory of that night in the car replays in my mind: the common blue orchid brooch, the fear in her eyes, the way she flattened it against the dash. Was that forced on her?

I close my eyes. Up in my office, I dig out my ancient laptop, determined to piece together everything. My office light flickers, and the computer fan whirs. Searching Chloe's name leads me down a rabbit hole: her mother's abrupt disappearance, therapy rumors, the canceled graduate program. Countless photos of Chloe next to her father at press events—no partners in any shot, no real glimpses of normal life. The deeper I scroll, the more my chest constricts. She was never free to be just Chloe Scott. Always someone's puppet or perfect image. I can practically feel her suffocation through these headlines.

By the time dawn bleeds pink across the windows, my eyes ache. I sit there, phone in hand, fighting an impulse to call her. Fear tangles my thoughts: what if everything's been a lie? But a pang of empathy overtakes me. Maybe I judged too fast. If I back away now, does that make me any different from the people who walked out on me?

A sudden thump in the bar below jolts me. I hear the door open. My heart leaps. I pad downstairs, gripping the banister. Sure enough, she's there. Chloe. Pale sunlight glints off her coat. She glances back at the door like she might flee. I can't ignore how her shoulders sag, exhaustion rolling off her in waves.

I manage to speak, voice husky. "You don't have to run," I say. "Not everyone bolts when the lights get harsh." The words come out more tender than I expect. She freezes, eyes swimming with relief and pain. Then her shoulders begin to shake. The door eases shut behind her, sealing us in the hush of the empty bar.

A tension pulses between us. I don't step closer yet, waiting to see if she'll vanish. But she lingers, fists clenched at her sides. I nod toward a lonely barstool. "Sit, if you want." Her eyes brim with unspoken apologies. I hold my breath, praying she doesn't slip away again.

Chapter Twelve

Chloe

I've never felt this vulnerable in my life. The bar is still, bathed in warm amber from the pendant lights overhead. No one else here, no background chatter. Lou stands behind the counter, arms folded, face guarded but not closed off. I rub the ache in my chest, the spot where my father's threats used to crush me, and realize I can't hold the lie any longer.

I set my purse down, gather courage, and let it pour out. "My father gave me a brooch," I say, voice unsteady. "but it's really a microphone. He threatened to freeze funding for my literacy program and lock me behind security if I refused."

Lou's eyes flare with recognition. Her posture shifts, loosening. "So that's why you avoided the bar," she says quietly. "So he wouldn't record us?"

I nod. My entire body trembles with a mixture of shame and relief. "Yes. I tried to keep his range useless. That's why I dragged you all over town. I never wanted to spy on you. For a while, I panicked, thinking you'd leave me. So I shut down." My throat tightens. "I'm sorry for not telling you."

Her expression softens, a thousand questions flickering there, but no accusation. I dig into my coat pocket, retrieve the common blue orchid brooch. It sparkles mockingly. My hand shakes so bad I nearly drop it. "I don't want it anymore," I whisper. "I'm done being his pawn."

I glance at the row of shot glasses behind the bar. Lou silently places one in front of me, amber reposado swirling within. I drop the brooch into the tequila and watch it sink. A fizz of tiny sparks erupts, the hidden electronics reacting. Without breaking eye contact, I lift the heavy shaker and bring the base down on it. The glass cracks, tequila splashes, and the brooch crumples under the blow. For one glorious second, I feel every tether to my father's oversight snap.

My hands tremble. "You're the only person who ever saw me," I say, voice cracking. "Not the headlines. Not the brand. Just me."

Lou stares at the destroyed brooch, breath coming quickly. She sets both hands on the bar. I reach across. Our fingers tangle, no more secrets between us.

We come together in a tentative kiss. It starts soft—a testing of waters—then grows urgent. Two days of heartbreak unravel in that press of lips. She slides around the bar, pulling me close, and I can't stop shaking from sheer relief.

The pendant lights catch the shine of tears on her lashes. I cling to her jacket, her warm presence steadier than anything I've known. She murmurs my name, voice husky. Then her hands find my waist. A current of longing surges. The kiss deepens, tongues brushing, breath mingling. My head spins, but I don't care. We stumble against the bar. I catch the faint aroma of cinnamon smoke on her collar.

Her lips move to my neck. My pulse skitters. I let out a small, desperate sound. She hoists me onto the bar, my legs wrapping around her hips. Our kisses turn frantic. I shiver at the scrape of denim against my thighs. I loosen her collar, trailing fingertips over her tattoos, savoring the tension coiled beneath her skin. Her mouth claims mine again, deeper this time.

"No holding back" effortlessly tumbles from her lips, and the intensity in her eyes cuts off my breath. She rocks forward, urging my hips to meet hers. I do, disastrously conscious of how easy this is. Of how right.

My hands memorize the smooth slope of her back, committing to muscle and bone. This is the final truce, the absolution I've ached for. The grip of her fingers finds my bruises and turns them to pleasure. Pain and pleasure, pleasure and pain—she's made a kindle of my nerves and I'm helpless to anything but the exquisite arch of her against me.

There's no real beginning or end. A tangle of seeking hands and soft gasps and clumsy cant of our bodies. It's carnal relief mixed with reverence, desperation and tenderness slamming together in staggering waves. When she spills over the edge, she chokes out my name like both a prayer and a weapon.

I tumble gratefully after, lost in the wash of blissful, biting electricity. Coming down, I'm drunk on her skin and my own clumsy ardor. She drapes herself across my chest with a shuddery sigh, our chests heaving in tandem. I can feel a smile curling into my hair.

"You and I," she murmurs, long after it would be prudent to back away. "This..." Punctuated with presses of her lips to my jaw. "I'm not sure if this was the best mistake of my life or the worst, but it was demonstrably not a choice."

I smooth a strand of hair from her forehead. "Definitely the best," I say, and I tug her back in, consequences be damned.

Much later, I'm draped in her oversized denim work shirt, the tail just long enough to cover me. The bar smells like tequila, sweat, faint cologne, and a promise I've never felt before. My legs still feel unsteady, heartbeat loud in my ears. Lou's leaning back, half-dressed, watching me with hooded eyes. The overhead lights flicker, revealing her flushed cheeks, the lines of her arms.

A silly grin spreads across my face. I slip off the bar, ignoring the ghost of nerves in my stomach. My father's prying eyes are gone. It's just us now. I meander to the shelves of liquor, rummaging for honey and bourbon. She cocks an eyebrow. "You know your way around a bottle?"

"Long story," I say, measuring a splash of bourbon, a spoonful of honey, a dash of cayenne. "My father hired a private chef when I was a teenager. I used to bribe him to show me normal things—like making real drinks—for the nights I was alone."

Lou watches closely, her mouth curving in appreciation. I shake the makeshift cocktail until the honey dissolves. Then I pour two glasses, presenting one to her with a flourish. She takes a sip, eyes going wide at the kick of cayenne. "You're full of surprises," she murmurs, voice warm.

I walk around the bar to where the crushed brooch lies in the broken shot glass. Carefully, she pinches the ruined pearls in a cloth, then hunts through a box of keepsakes near the register. She retrieves a yellowed postcard featuring a '66 Thunderbird. I recognize the faint cursive scrawl that must belong to her mother. Gently, Lou slides the battered postcard closer. Then she pins the melted remains of the brooch beside it, tiny wires glinting under the overhead light.

She grabs a pen, scribbles across a piece of tape, and pastes it above the pinned items. The label reads: PROOF WE STAY. I stare, tears pricking my eyes again. The bar has always represented her refuge—and a prison. Now she's letting me stand in her safe place, forging a piece of me into its history.

We clink our glasses. The bourbon coats my tongue with sweet heat, and she meets my gaze. "You sure about staying?" she asks softly, a hint of vulnerability shining through.

I brush back a stray lock of her hair. "It's the only thing I'm certain of." and this time, it doesn't feel like a trap. It feels like strength. The decision is mine. Not my father's, not the tabloids'. Mine.

Epilogue

Lou

Strands of carnival lights buzz overhead. The sidewalk outside The Getaway bristles with folding tables, neon banners, and scuffed karaoke speakers that I've tested five times already. Kids dash by, shrieking about funnel cakes. Vendors holler about fresh lemonade. All around me, Fairford's Founders Day festival throbs with life, so loud and bright it rattles my insides like a live wire. I grin at the chaos while hugging a clipboard against my chest. Emceeing this karaoke charity contest was Bobby's idea, but I volunteered to run with it the moment he asked. My bar is more than a watering hole tonight—it's the stage for a carnival turned block party. Chasing a frayed mic cord, I dodge a couple in matching T-shirts who gush, "Lou, can't wait to sing that Lady Gaga song!" I wave back, adrenaline stoking my nerves. I can almost taste the electric tension in the air.

Inside The Getaway, it's standing room only. Outside, we've set up a makeshift bar beneath a rainbow-striped canopy. Avery, from across the street at the bakery, slides me a bottled water. My throat's already scratchy from calling out raffle numbers and encouraging nervous singers who forget their lyrics halfway through. No fiascos yet, though. The festival crowd tips well, especially when they see we're donating proceeds to a battered-women's shelter. I catch a glimpse of Chloe manning her dunk-tank booth two tents over. She's wearing a T-shirt that reads READERS ARE REBELS, and she's got this playful grin as she coaxes passersby to take aim at the target. Her laughter drifts my way. It hits me square in the chest, like her voice always does. Eight months ago, I would've kept my distance, worried intimacy was a mirage. Now, I can't imagine going a second without her in my sight.

I tap the microphone, signal that we're pausing karaoke for a special announcement, and watch Chloe step forward. She slides me a nod, then takes the mic with a steady hand. The crowd quiets fast. Apparently, the mayor's about to arrive, and the sea of reporters ripple at the edges. Chloe wears that calm face I've seen at her father's press events, but there's a flicker in her eyes.

She starts slow. Talks about community outreach, about real leadership meaning accountability. When she thanks her father for demonstrating what leadership isn't, the hush in the crowd morphs into a collective gasp. Then she looks right into a camera lens and says, "I'd like to endorse a candidate, not because they're my father's adversary, but because they'll sign the ethics bill he vetoed." Her voice doesn't shake.

Reporters raise phones and microphones, shouting questions that slam together like hailstones. Chloe glances at Stevie, who's stationed behind the local news crew. He gives her a brief nod and mouths, "Keep going." She thanks him and continues. This time her words hold an undercurrent of relief. She's cutting the last tether to her father's brand, stepping into her own. Her father emerges from behind a stack of crates, stony-faced. Cameras swivel. He doesn't interrupt, but the tension makes the air taste metallic. Chloe recognizes it too. I can read it in her posture—those shoulders squared, the pulse at her temple. She signs off with one last line about how foundations should serve the people, not bury them in spin. Then she thanks everyone for listening, hands me the mic, and steps back. Stevie meets her halfway, wraps an arm around her, and I see tears shining in his eyes.

I can still feel the crackle in the atmosphere as I usher the karaoke volunteers back on stage. The show must go on, so we keep collecting donations for the shelter. Over an hour later, I announce the winner—some fearless teenager who belted out a Whitney Houston ballad like it was second nature.

By the time I step away from the mic, my voice is raw, and the festival's started winding down. That's when I catch Chloe's eye from across the street. She tucks a stray hair behind her ear and waves me over. My own grin feels unstoppable as I weave through the thinning crowd. Her father and the cameras are gone, leaving behind a swirl of rumor. But Chloe stands there, radiant with relief, free from that veneer of caution. Before I can speak, she loops an arm around my waist and draws me in for a quick kiss.

I steer her toward a corner near the bar's outdoor patio, where half the crowd has gathered around tall tables.

Bobby, who's dressed in a flower-print jumpsuit and cowboy boots, notices our approach and hollers, "All good back here, boss, but you're on tap duty tomorrow!" I grin, grateful that Bobby's got my back.

Then I turn to Chloe and say, "Speaking of tomorrow, I've got something to show you tonight." She arches a brow. Instead of explaining, I fish a key fob out of my front pocket. I gently press it into her palm. She studies the cracked plastic emblem, some classic car silhouette battered with time. No answer—just an inquisitive tilt of her head. My heart pounds. I duck out into the side alley, leading her toward the storage lot behind The Getaway. Her footsteps slow as the shape of a '66 Thunderbird gleams under a string of bulbs.

I bought the shell at a salvage auction in Indianapolis. For months, I worked on it after closing time, coaxing each stubborn piece of metal back into working order. The paint is a muted teal, not glossy, but the body lines are strong enough to make me dizzy with pride. Chloe breathes out a quiet "Wow."

I step closer, open the passenger door, and say, "Gonna name him Scott." Chloe slides into the seat, trailing her fingers over the glove box.

She whispers, "Your mother's dream car." I nod. My chest feels tight. I can't change the past or recoup what she stole from me, but I can reclaim what I love about that fantasy: the open road, the idea of taking life beyond the horizon. The trunk is already packed with a battered suitcase and blank postcards for The Getaway's memory wall. This time, it's a road trip for two.

With Chloe still seated, I fish something else from my back pocket. A tiny resin cube on a thin silver chain. Clear epoxy with a milky swirl at its center. It's a shard of that brooch the private investigator had melted down. She stares, confusion flickering over her face until I say, "I saved this piece. Just as a reminder; with mme, you always have a choice" I slip the chain around her neck. The resin catches the string lights like a prism. She inhales sharply. I notice the slight tremor in her fingers as she touches the pendant. Then, with a small smile, she digs into her backpack and pulls out a flask of reposado tequila. "Thought we might want to toast," she murmurs, popping the top. I grin.

Darkness settles over Fairford, but the festival lights glow brighter than the stars. I glance at my watch. Almost midnight. Perfect time to hit the road. Bobby's behind the bar, counting tips, and throws me a salute as we roll the Thunderbird onto the main street. The engine rattles, not fully restored, but it's enough to carry us forward. Chloe's hair sways in the breeze through the missing passenger window. My collarbone hums where her breath lingers from a kiss moments ago. We pass the flickering neon sign of The Getaway.

I turn left at the corner, feeling an exhilaration I never allowed myself before. Chloe's hand rests on my thigh.. I press the gas, and the car responds.

We drive straight for the county road, where the streetlights end and the farmland begins. Our trunk brims with postcards waiting for new stories. The leftover tip jar rattles with a few bills and coins, each clink a promise of possibility. Chloe flips through the radio stations until she finds some classic rock tune and we let it fill the empty darkness. I can't help glancing over at her every few seconds. Her eyes shin. My heart aches in the best way. All I want is to keep going, to let the miles stretch behind us like. The T-bird's old engine sputters, but it keeps going, same as us. In the side mirror, Fairford shrinks into darkness. Ahead, the open road beckons, ours for as long as we dare to chase it.

Chapter One

♥

Kari

My heart pounds so hard it might crack a rib. I'm standing in my editor's office, ignoring the faint whiff of burned coffee and last night's takeout. I've just been handed a file folder with a name that makes my stomach flip: Everleigh Taylor. The Everleigh Taylor, socialite royalty, rumored to be as glamorous as she is unattainable. Apparently, my first cover story for CityLine won't be a cozy lifestyle piece about local coffee carts after all.

"Honestly, Kari, this is a huge deal." My editor, Paula, smacks the folder lightly against her desk. "They don't hand out interviews with Leigh Taylor every day."

I try not to fidget. "I appreciate the opportunity, Paula, honestly, but I—"

"You're the best we have." She waves away my protest. "And you're due for something big. You have it in you."

I swallow. "I appreciate that, really. But... have you seen anything I've written lately? I do introspective column stuff, short interviews with yoga instructors. You're throwing me into shark-infested water here."

"Don't be dramatic," she snips. "I can always assign it to Peterson." She spins around, scanning the cluttered office for the new hire. I stiffen. Peterson? He's barely been here for two weeks. And with the amount of times he's gotten our coffee orders wrong, he's practically an intern. There's no way he has the got to take on a cover story. especially not one with this much clout.

She catches my expression and arches a brow. "So, you taking it or not?"

I let out a resigning sigh. "I'll take it." My voice wavers. "But if this goes south—"

"You'll make it work." She doesn't let me finish. "You have a meet-and-greet at Taylor Foundation headquarters tomorrow. Preparatory interview. Maybe a photo op, if you're lucky."

One quick nod, and I exit her office, hugging the folder to my chest. Leigh Taylor. An impossible subject. She's rumored to be cold, private, and controlled. She's also rumored to have a forced engagement on the horizon, but I'm not sure if that's just a gossip rag special. I guess I'll find out soon.

***

By the time I reach the Taylor Foundation building, I'm running five minutes behind schedule. The driver who was supposed to drop me at the entrance got lost, so I spent an extra three minutes scurrying around this part of town—where the architecture is sleek, glassy, and intimidating.. It's a far cry from my quiet apartment building a few neighborhoods over.

I hustle inside, where an overly polished receptionist asks me to wait. The lobby is an enormous expanse of polished marble, with wide windows facing a courtyard fountain. Modern, but somehow clinical. I shift my weight in front of her desk, clutching my tote bag.

Finally, an assistant glides out from a side corridor, impeccable in a black skirt and a crisp blouse. She greets me with a professional half-smile. "Kari Marsdon? Ms. Taylor will see you now. I'm Jessie."

"Nice to meet you, Jessie," her handshake is firm, but her smile is kinder than anything I expected when I walked into this building.

" Of course. Right this way Miss."

I follow her, weaving through hallways that smell like new carpet and lemon-scented air freshener. Jessie leads me into a private meeting room. The moment I cross the threshold, my shoulders tense.

Leigh Taylor sits at a long, gleaming table, posture perfect, hands resting lightly on the surface. Her dark hair slides over one shoulder in a silky sweep. Tall. Elegant. Her eyes are guarded, a smoky gray or maybe deep brown. I can't quite tell from across the room.

"Good morning," she says. Her voice is low, clipped. She extends her hand, and I shake it, noticing how her skin is cool but firm. No nonsense. Just a tiny angle to her chin that suggests a challenge. Dares me to prove I'm worthy of her time.

I set up my phone to record, but before I can begin, she withdraws slightly. Jessie stands behind her, tapping on a tablet. Leigh waits. Her eyes flick to the phone.

Right. She expects me to lead. "Thanks for meeting with me, Ms. Taylor," I begin. "I appreciate you setting aside the time."

She nods. "Leigh is fine."

There's no warmth, just polite detachment. She crosses her legs, the fabric of her tailored pants immaculate. I open my folder.

"We have thirty minutes," she says. "The official quote and images are available through my office. Jessie will handle that. Let's keep this concise."

Concise. Sure. "Understood." I press the record button. "This cover story is slated to run in CityLine's next issue. We're looking to get a personal perspective. A glimpse beyond the usual corporate angle."

Her lips curve into something resembling a smile, but it doesn't soften her eyes. "I see."

"Perhaps we can start with your role as COO of the Taylor Foundation's philanthropic branch," I suggest, feeling a rush of self-consciousness. "The city's curious about your recent initiative—"

She cuts in with an answer that sounds eerily memorized: "At the Taylor Foundation, we focus on harnessing the synergy between energy innovation and social responsibility. We aim to address Foundation challenges by—"

I wait for something real, but all I get is polished media speak. It spills out as if she's reading from a teleprompter. My shoulders sink. I ask a follow-up question, hoping to catch her off-guard.

She rattles off more bullet points, not missing a beat. I grit my teeth. I get it: She's used to controlling her own narrative, and I'm a potential threat. But this is nothing more than a rehash of her press releases.

I keep trying, anyway. "So, on a personal note, do you—"

Before I can finish, the door swings open. Jessie rushes in, eyes wide. "Ms. Taylor, there's...a situation."

Leigh's expression tightens. "What sort of situation?"

"The greenhouse." Jessie blurts out. "A squirrel, it, um, got in somehow and is...chewing up the Queen of the Night."

Leigh bolts to her feet, curses under her breath. It's quiet, but I catch the slip. She glances my way, then turns to Jessie. "Show me."

They head for the door. I scramble after them, my bag bouncing off my hip. "Are we—where—?"

"This way," Jessie calls back, stepping into an elevator across the hall. "We need to get upstairs."

I slip between the sliding doors at the last second, ignoring the sting of fury in Leigh's eyes. She seems irritated that I'm tagging along. But I can't pass up the chance to see her in an unscripted moment.

When the elevator dings, we spill out onto the top floor. It's eerily quiet up here. No bustling assistants, no staff chatter. Just massive windows letting in bright light. Jessie leads us to a set of double doors, and Leigh punches in a code. The doors open, revealing a lush greenhouse that practically glows with humidity and warmth.

I step inside, inhaling the earthy sweetness of living plants—a world away from the sterile building below. Potted orchids line the tables, roses climb the walls, and ferns dangle overhead. Moss and bright succulents crowd together in decorative arrangements.

Leigh storms past me, scanning the rows of pots. "Where is it?"

Jessie points behind a cluster of exotic orchids. I see a twitch of motion—tiny, furry, a trembling shape nibbling on a leaf. A squirrel? Some other little rodent? Hard to tell.

Leigh edges closer. The creature flinches. Then it darts off, scattering pebbles and nearly toppling a pot of black-petaled flowers. Jessie lunges but misses. I let out an involuntary laugh as she *splats* on the floor.

Leigh shoots me a steely glance. I clamp my mouth shut. She steps gingerly between the tables, trying to corner the invader. I circle around the other side, hoping to help. The succulent tables are cramped. My foot bumps a terracotta pot. I wince. A scattering of potting soil hits the ground.

"Sorry," I whisper, inching sideways. Ahead, Leigh crouches behind a tall stack of purple-streaked orchids, her shoulders rolling slowly like a cat on the prowl. Jessie flaps her arms, trying to herd the panicked critter toward the door.

The creature makes a break for it, squeaks under a table, and barrels toward the exit. Leigh leaps in its path, startling it again. It whips around, scurries over my sneaker, and disappears through the open doors.

Jessie exhales loudly. I gape at Leigh but she barely seems phased. She straightens, dusting bits of mulch off her pants, paying no mind to the dirt on her hands.

"That's that," she mutters. Then she sees the damage: snapped stems, torn leaves, and scattered petals. Some of the pots have rolled onto their sides, exposing roots and sending soil across the floor.

"I'll grab a dustpan," Jessie murmurs.

As Jessie scurries out, Leigh eyes the battered flowers in front of her. Gently, she hoists a tilting orchid upright and sets the pot on a sturdy surface. I notice the tender way she cradles the stem, how she pats the dirt back into place. Her entire demeanor has changed from dangerous ice sculpture to dedicated caretaker. It's mesmerizing.

I step forward, only half aware I'm still clutching my phone. "Need help?"

She looks at me like it's the last thing she expected to hear. "You want to help with my...flowers?"

I nod. "They're beautiful." I lean in, sniffing a large orchid bloom. "And I read somewhere that you have a fondness for them. Secretly a green thumb?"

A flicker of amusement crosses her face. "Didn't realize that was public knowledge."

"It's not," I admit softly. "I just found one old article quoting your father. He mentioned his daughter liked gardening."

Something about that mention of family shutters her expression again. But she doesn't refuse me. She takes a stack of small plastic containers from a shelf and begins clearing away the damaged pieces. I watch her lift a pot containing a black orchid with curled petals. She sighs when she sees the cracks in the ceramic.

"Is that the Queen of the Night?" I ask, recalling what Jessie said.

She nods. "They bloom only occasionally. Fussy." Her tone holds a weird tenderness. "My favorite."

I help by gathering spilled soil. It's warm to the touch. An earthy smell rises. I glimpse Leigh's face as she tries to repot a drooping orchid, and for the first time since I arrived, she looks relaxed. My recorder is still running, but I'm not sure if I should keep going or let this moment be private.

"Hand me that scoop," she says. The words are polite but brisk.

I pass it over, and we settle into a surprisingly comfortable rhythm. She checks roots, I steady pots. It's quiet enough that I hear her soft breathing. Tiny glints of sweat bead along her hairline from the greenhouse's humidity.

She glances up, catches my gaze. "You've gone off script, Ms. Marsdon."

My cheeks warm. "Sorry. I just—I wanted something authentic. Not the usual brand spiel."

She presses her lips together, as though waging an internal debate. Then, with a thin smile, "You're planting flowers with me. That's not typical for a Taylor interview."

I give a tiny shrug. "I'll take whatever I can get."

She exhales. Something like a laugh. "Fine. Careful with that stem."

"Right." I gingerly shift the orchid into a new pot. The green swirls of its leaves brush my wrist. "What made you build a greenhouse up here? I mean, plant conservation is not exactly your company's main mission."

"Exactly," she says. She dusts dirt off her palm and leans against the table. "That's kind of the point. This place...no one really checks. I get some privacy." She raises an eyebrow, as if daring me to mock her.

I shake my head. "Privacy from what?"

She lifts one shoulder. "Everything."

Her expression flickers, like she's not used to vulnerability—her own or anyone else's. She moves on, rummaging for a fresh bag of soil. I help her hold the next pot steady. My forearm brushes hers, and a slight current of awareness travels up my spine. She must feel it, too, because she clears her throat abruptly.

I swallow. My voice comes out softer than I expect. "Will you show me how to cut an orchid stem properly?"

Her gaze shoots to mine. "You're serious?"

I grin, a bit nervous. "I don't want to accidentally kill one by trimming incorrectly. I'd like to learn."

She hesitates, perhaps gauging if I'm mocking her. Then she picks up a pair of pruning shears and demonstrates, guiding my hand. Her fingers settle over mine, and we slice at a precise angle. The stem falls away, leaving a neat edge for new growth. I realize how close we're standing, shoulders nearly touching. I inhale the subtle trace of her perfume, an undercurrent of fresh citrus.

"So you come here often?"

Her lips quirk. "I tend these personally. Yes. No interns. No staff."

"Why?" I ask, ignoring the beeping in my head that warns me I'm skipping every essential bullet from my editor's list.

She exhales softly—a near-silent laugh, maybe. "I don't trust outsiders with something fragile. The margin for error is too high."

My heart tugs. Fragile. Check. Fear of letting people see the vulnerability. Double check. I glance at my scribbled notes—my handwriting is a mess. "So you're protective?"

She steps back from the cabinet, crossing her arms again. "Is that your conclusion?"

"Well, you called them delicate. You said you don't let others handle them. That suggests you find them precious. Something you'd rather keep safe."

She steps back first. My hand tingles where she was touching it. "Any other questions?"

I want to ask a million. But I bite my tongue. "Let's start with why you love flowers so much. Why these plants, especially?"

She considers for a moment. Then in a quiet tone, she says, "They remind me that life needs nurturing. Growth doesn't happen by accident—it's a choice you make every day, whether you realize it or not."

That knocks me off-balance. Maybe because I know what it means to be alone, trying to cultivate something that keeps you going. "That's...that's really something," I manage finally.

She's about to elaborate when Jessie bursts back into the greenhouse. Her tablet clatters, and she's panting. "Ms. Taylor, your mother just arrived downstairs. She's expecting an update. Apparently, she wants to ensure your meeting is on track."

Leigh's eyes go cold. The softness vanishes like a snapped thread. She sets down the pruning shears. "I have to go."

I gather my notebook and phone, following Leigh and Jessie out of the greenhouse in a hurry. We take the elevator back down, and I notice Leigh's entire posture shift. Shoulders squared, chin up, face unreadable. It's so abrupt I almost miss the warm gaze she had just a minute ago.

In the hallway, Felicity Taylor waits. She's impeccably dressed in a pencil skirt and designer blazer. Poise radiates off her in waves. Her eyes narrow on Leigh, and then flick to me, likely judging me in a single glance.

"There you are, darling," Felicity says, her tone smooth. "And this must be Ms. Marsdon from CityLine." She extends a polite but distant hand, and I shake it.

"Nice to meet you, Mrs. Taylor." My skin prickles under her scrutiny.

"And you," she replies, forcing a brittle smile. "I trust this interview is going well? We want to ensure we're painting the Taylor brand in a positive light."

Leigh stiffens. The micro-shift in her expression is like a rose snapping shut. A moment ago, I glimpsed the woman behind the brand. Now, I see the polished figure in a high-stakes chess game.

Leigh inclines her head. "We were just wrapping up."

Felicity's eyes snap to me. "I see. I do hope you're highlighting the philanthropic angle in your piece, Ms. Marsdon. It's crucial. The Taylor brand encompasses more than just profits; we're about shaping the community."

I swallow, trying to keep my expression polite. "That was the plan," I say gently, even though I suspect we're about to be steered far, far away from the hint of vulnerability I'd just discovered in Leigh.

Leigh hesitates, then excuses herself in a low voice. "I'll walk you out, Mother."

But Felicity shakes her head. "Don't be silly. Ms. Marsdon, if you have a moment, why don't you join me in my office? We can extend your interview. Get the official perspective, ensure the brand is captured accurately."

I catch the slightly panicked flicker in Leigh's gaze, as if she wants to intervene. But Felicity is already ushering me toward the door. Jess stands at the threshold, eyes darting between mother and daughter. Leigh tries to voice an objection—something about "We haven't covered everything Ms. Marsdon needed." But Felicity dismisses it with a wave.

Felicity leads me down the corridor into a spacious office suite, the kind with double doors and a conference table that seats twelve. Floor-to-ceiling windows showcase the city's skyline. Coffee is served with a snap of her finger at an assistant who scurries away.

Felicity sits behind her massive desk, gestures for me to take the sleek leather chair, and invites Leigh to stand or sit. Leigh moves behind me, half out of my line of sight.

Felicity smiles. "We're delighted you're doing a feature on my daughter's achievements. So many women must be inspired by her example."

My stomach twists. The conversation has pivoted to full-blown corporate spin, exactly what my editor claims sells magazines. But the reason I became a journalist years ago was to find truth in the mundane, not be a PR echo chamber.

I try to start on neutral ground. "Your daughter's philanthropic efforts are impressive. I was just learning about her interest in horticulture."

Felicity's mouth pinches. "That's a small hobby. Not the headline. You should focus on her real achievements: the expansion of our tech solutions, the philanthropic partnerships overseas, her upcoming wedding that will unite two crucial families in our industry. That's the story the public needs."

Leigh's shoulders tense. She looks almost smaller here than in the greenhouse. "Mother," she says gently. "Ms. Marsdon has her own approach."

Felicity ignores the hint of protest. "We must keep the conversation on brand. People admire the Taylors for philanthropy, industriousness, tradition. Wouldn't you agree, Ms. Marsdon?"

I force a smile. "I'm sure that's a key part. But my column focuses on the human side of success. Readers want to feel connected."

Felicity lifts her chin, eyebrows arching elegantly. "Well, if you insist on something more personal, we can incorporate a few carefully chosen details—like how Leigh's fiancé shares our philanthropic vision. Isn't that right, darling?"

Leigh's eyes flick to me. There's a weight there, as if she's silently apologizing. Then she inclines her head. "Yes. Giles and I are aligned on many charitable fronts."

Leigh stands still as stone, letting her mother talk. I see it—the ninety-degree pivot from greenhouse caretaker to corporate ice queen's daughter. She's quiet, watchful, letting Felicity run the show.

Felicity commands the conversation, firing off details about philanthropic alliances, big donors, upcoming expansions. Leigh sits to her right, expression locked in place.

I attempt to ask Leigh direct questions—about her personal drive, her experiences. Each time, Felicity interjects with a curated response. She references press releases, brand statements, corporate agendas. Leigh occasionally offers a tiny sentence, but she doesn't expand. She doesn't deviate from the script. It's like listening to a ventriloquist act.

Minutes turn into an hour. My eyes flick to the clock. Leigh must see my tension, because she fidgets with a pen. Then Jessie pops her head in, face contrite. "I'm sorry to interrupt, Mrs. Taylor, but Ms. Taylor has another important meeting scheduled."

Felicity's lips tighten. She checks her watch. "So be it. Very well. Ms. Marsdon, we must wrap up." She stands, extending her hand again. "I trust we've given you plenty."

Plenty of corporate spin, sure. But not the real Leigh Taylor that I caught a glimpse of upstairs. I gather my notes with a forced smile. "Thank you for your time."

Leigh rises, offering only the faintest smile. "I'll walk you out."

Together, we leave her mother's office. Once outside, I can almost feel the tension crackle. Leigh glances around to make sure no one's listening. Then she exhales. "I'm sorry about all that."

I try to stay professional. "I completely understand. She just wants to protect the brand."

Leigh's face clouds. "Right," she says flatly. Then she looks away, expression distant. I see something flicker in her eyes—disappointment, regret? Before I can decode it, it vanishes behind a practiced mask. "Anyway," she continues, voice calm, "I know this probably isn't the angle your editor asked for."

I shake my head. "It's...it's fine. Really."

She holds up a hand to stop me. "Jessie?"

Her assistant steps forward, rummaging in her sleek bag. She produces a glossy pass on a lanyard. It reads BACKSTAGE ACCESS – PODCAST SUMMIT.

Leigh hands it to me with a guarded tilt. "I'm speaking at a podcast interview tomorrow. Tech meets rural communities. You'll have free rein behind the scenes. Maybe that'll give you what you need—and spare us another endless Q&A with my mother."

I'm stunned but try to keep my cool. "Thank you." I tuck the pass into my tote. "I'll be there."

She nods, stepping to the curb outside the building. A sleek car waits for her. "I'll see you tomorrow, then."

My mind spins with so many questions. I want to ask about that greenhouse, about her early life, about the fiancé rumor. But I bite my tongue. "Thank you again," I say, mustering a nervous smile. "I appreciate the chance."

She nods and prepares to climb into the car. Before she does, she glances at me over her shoulder. The corner of her mouth twitches—like she might smile. Then she clamps it down, the armor snapping back into place.

I stand there, traffic rumbling, wind drifting through the tall buildings. My notebook feels heavy in my arms. I replay the memory of how her face softened when we saved that orchid. The care in her voice when she said that growth doesn't happen by accident. It's a fleeting glimpse of who she really is. And I'm not sure if I imagined it.

The car door slams, and her driver pulls into the bustle of midday traffic. I watch them go until I can't see the license plate anymore. Then I let out a shaky breath, rummaging for my phone. My editor's definitely going to want an update.

But before I can call her my phone buzzes with a text. "Heard you spent the day with Felicity. She's a handful, huh? Where's the scoop?"

I close my eyes, leaning my head back. The scoop is that I'm in trouble if I can't deliver a compelling piece. Right now, I'm not sure if I've got enough. But tomorrow's my second chance. And I can't deny I'm... intrigued by Leigh. The way she changed in her mother's presence was startling, but it also piqued my curiosity. She's not the stiff figure the tabloids paint her to be. She's lonely, maybe. Protective. Definitely used to wearing armor.

I text back: "Interview with Leigh tomorrow. Might get better material. Will draft after that."

My editor responds with a thumbs-up emoji and a short "Don't hold back."

I sigh, staring at the message. The day started with carefully curated lines and half-lies. But in that greenhouse, we had a moment. I saw the Leigh behind the Taylor name. I wonder if it'll happen again tomorrow or if I'll be back to bullet points and brand management.

I know one thing: This story won't be as simple as I'd hoped.

The Vows We Break

The feature was meant to polish Leigh Taylor's image— not torch her fake fairy-tale engagement.

Heiress and philanthropic powerhouse Leigh Taylor has been publicly "betrothed" to childhood friend Giles Hennessy for ten carefully scripted months. The arrangement pleases donors, pacifies her mother, and keeps the Taylor Foundation's billion-dollar expansion on track. Leigh just has to smile through fittings, flash the ring, and pretend she isn't suffocating.

Enter journalist Kari Marsdon, desperate for her first cover story at *CityLine* Magazine. Shadowing Chicago's golden couple should be safe, splashy copy—until Leigh's quick wit and hidden vulnerability turn every interview into electrified banter. Late-night fact-checks morph into clandestine Thai take-out, and Kari begins to see the woman—not the headline—beneath the perfect up-do.

When Kari's article hits newsstands, it's an instant sensation...and a land mine. Leigh's mother spins the piece as "miscommunication," board members freeze pledges, and Giles—feeling the spotlight shift—leaks a statement claiming Leigh was *overwhelmed* and *off-message*. To salvage years of planning, the Taylor Foundation unleashes damage control that demands one brutal fix: move the wedding date up and put Leigh back in her crystal cage.

Leigh refuses to lose the only person who's ever seen her, yet stepping off the gilded path could detonate her family's legacy. Kari can clear Leigh's name, but exposing the newsroom politics—and the publicity-stunt engagement—might end the career she's fought to claim.

When vows to family, ambition, and a fabricated fiancé collide with the vows of the heart, which promises will they dare to keep...and which ones will they break?

Preorder Now

Thank you

♥

Thanks for joining me on this adventure. Book reviews from awesome readers like you are the lifeblood of authors. If you enjoyed the book, please take a moment to leave a review; you'd be surprised how much it helps! If you want to be the first to know about the other romances in this collection, visit: www.halfcaffpress.com to subscribe to my newsletter and gain access to behind-the-scenes tidbits and get early glimpses at all of my upcoming projects.

Also by Claerie Kavanaugh

O Once Upon a Love Story

Happily Ever Afters aren't just for fairy tales.

Ember Davenport made a promise to herself: graduate debt-free from NYU. She pays her dues as a party princess and is perfectly happy with her busy, love-free life. When her roommate begs her to be a guinea pig for her new matchmaking website, she chalks it up as an easy favor to a good friend. Afterall, what's the worst that can happen?

As the youngest casting director in Manhattan, Layla Crawford has the life everyone dreams of when they move to the Big Apple. Famous actors fear her, all the tabloids know her name, and she somehow landed her dream job only two years post-graduation. Too bad she doesn't have anyone to share it with.

Neither of them expects anything to come out of signing up for Matches Ever After. But a single swipe right might just change their lives for good.

This is the first novella in the standalone romance series Entertaining Love. Click the link you sign up for my newsletter and read it for FREE!

Love Among the Stars: A Matchmaker Romance

Hollywood's best matchmaker may have finally met her match.

Genevieve "Eve" Davis is Hollywood's best, most sought-after matchmaker. Just about in the City of Angels owes her for their happily ever afters. She's been in the business for ten years and has never made a false move. The only person she hasn't been able to hit with Cupid's arrow? Herself.

Then Jemma, Hollywood's most recent "it" girl, shows up on her doorstep. But rather than having an extra bounce in her step, she looks like a dog just crapped all over her brand-new designer boots. The date Eve setup for her was anything but a fairytale beginning. It was a downright disaster. The first bad review Eve has ever had. If she can't fix this, her perfect reputation will be about as useful as an empty box of chocolates.

Even worse, the deeper she digs for that secret ingredient that will help her find Jemma's perfect match, the harder she falls.

Love On Page Six: A Secret Celebrity Romance

An actress with a secret, a journalist with a dream, and forbidden love that could change everything.

Desperate to save her family's dying magazine, love is the last thing on 26-year-old Daphne Fernandez's mind when she agrees to go undercover as a makeup artist to scoop a juicy story on the city's most popular telenovela star. But a spur-of-the-moment kiss makes it more complicated. A cheating boyfriend might not be Bombshell Bridget's only secret.

Bridget Blake has only ever wanted one thing in her life: to be herself. But her overbearing momanger insists showing the world who she really is would mean the death of her blossoming career. So when the new makeup artist fights her way under Bridget's perfectly moisturized, paparazzi-proof skin, it's everything she can do to keep the façade in place. Until one spontaneous kiss turns her world upside down. With Daphne, Bridget is the brave, fun-loving, take-no-prisoners girl she's always wanted to be. But embracing her new self may mean leaving behind everything she's ever worked for. Is love really worth it?

A DASH OF LOVE FOR CHRISTMAS

From anonymous chats to a whirlwind holiday romance—can love survive the spotlight?

Sage Holloway used to adore Christmas. But after a devastating breakup, the nurse finds herself dodging mistletoe and romantic entanglements in equal measure. Until a chance encounter with a single mom and her precocious daughter begins to thaw her heart.

Peyton "Pepper" Liu, a former celebrity chef, has traded the chaos of Hollywood for the cozy charm of Hollyvale. Determined to give her daughter a stable life, Pepper pours all her energy into opening her dream restaurant. Love isn't on the menu—until she crosses paths with Sage, whose grounded nature feels like a lifeline in Pepper's whirlwind world.

At the urging of their meddling friends, both women join *Matches Ever After*, a high-end matchmaking app. Unbeknownst to them, their anonymous chats spark a connection as electric as their real-life encounters. But as their bond deepens, so do the secrets Pepper keeps.

When a glittering holiday pageant turns into a media circus, Sage discovers Pepper's true identity—and the messy past she's been hiding.

Can Sage trust Pepper's intentions? Can Pepper prove she's more than the headlines? And can they find a way back to each other in time for Christmas?

Captured by Cupid (Cori & Zoe – Grumpy/Sunshine, Forced Proximity, Escape Room Romance)

An escape room, a meddling matchmaker, and one impossible-to-ignore attraction...

Cordelia "Cori" Daniels does *not* believe in love. The only thing worse than Valentine's Day? Being trapped in an over-the-top, romance-themed escape room with Zoe Valentine—the town's most relentless flirt and walking ball of sunshine.

Zoe is determined to crack Cori's icy exterior, even if it means pushing every button she has. But when the puzzles turn personal and the tension between them ignites, escaping might be the *last* thing either of them wants.

Grumpy x Sunshine

Enemies-ish to Lovers

Trapped Together in an Escape Room

A Meddling Matchmaker Who Won't Take No for an Answer

Can Zoe charm her way into Cori's heart, or will this escape room remain locked—for good?

Cuffed by Cupid *(Kendell &* *Morgan – Opposites Attract, Accidental Arrest, Small-Town Chaos)*

One pair of handcuffs, one bar fight gone wrong, and one very grumpy detective who is *not* amused...

Detective Kendell Kalloway has zero patience for troublemakers—especially not Morgan Harlow, the infuriatingly charming bartender who just got herself arrested. It's a *huge misunderstanding*, but thanks to a filing mishap, Morgan is stuck spending the night at Kendell's place.

Morgan sees this as a perfect opportunity—to push Kendell's buttons, flirt shamelessly, and maybe (just maybe) prove there's *something real* beneath all the bickering. But when small-town gossip, a Valentine's charity date auction, and a very determined matchmaker conspire to throw them together, Kendell might just be completely outmatched.

Grumpy x Chaos Gremlin

Forced Proximity (Oops, Only One Bed)

A Fake Date That's Definitely Not Fake

Will Kendell resist Morgan's relentless charm, or will this detective finally *surrender* to love?

Cornered by Cupid *(Iliana & Talia – Second Chance, Fake Dating, Forced Proximity Spa Retreat)*

They were each other's greatest love—until one of them walked away. Now? They're stuck pretending to be a couple...

Illiana Anderson has built a perfect life—her luxury spa retreat, her high-profile clients, her strictly single status. She *does not* have time for distractions—especially not Talia Harlow, the one who got away.

Talia never planned to return to Rosemont Ridge, but thanks to a scheming matchmaker, she's found herself stuck at Illiana's couples' retreat—as her *fake* girlfriend. It's supposed to be a harmless cover, just for the weekend.

Except the chemistry? Very real. And the way Talia looks at Illiana, like she's still the center of her universe? Even worse.

Second-Chance Romance

Fake Dating at a Luxury Spa Retreat

High-Stakes Couples Challenges (That Get Too Personal, Too Fast)

One Bed. Obviously.

When the past collides with the present, will Illiana and Talia finally get their happy ending—or is history doomed to repeat itself?

Caught by Cupid (Nova & Delilah—A Short Sapphic Matchmaker Gets Matched Enemies to Lovers Romance)

The matchmaker has finally met her match... and she's infuriatingly perfect.

Nova Valentine has made a career out of love—other people's, not her own. As the mastermind behind Casanova Connections, she's built an empire by predicting romantic tropes and engineering perfect matches. But when her latest clients (including her annoyingly happy friends) conspire to set her up with her biggest rival? Cupid can go choke on his arrows.

Delilah Sterling is too confident. Too polished. Too smug. And way too good at making Nova lose her cool.

They're supposed to be competitors, not a love story. But the sparks between them are impossible to ignore... and when a fake collaboration turns dangerously real, Nova starts to wonder if she's been playing the wrong game all along.

Now it's her heart on the line—and this time, she's not the one in control.

Tropes:

Matchmaker Gets Matched

Enemies-to-Lovers

Meddling Friends (and past book couples!)

Slow Burn, High Heat

Business Rivals with History

The Cupid Chronicles Omnibus

Love? Overrated. Until it isn't.

Welcome to Rosemont Ridge, where meddling matchmakers, romantic disasters, and accidental soulmates are all just part of the Valentine legacy.

In this swoony, sapphic rom-com series packed with grumpy girls, chaos gremlins, second chances, and slow-burn rivals-to-lovers sparks, one thing's for sure: no one escapes Cupid's grip... not even the matchmaker herself.

Includes all four sizzling novellas:

Captured by Cupid – A no-nonsense realist and a sunshine flirt get locked in a romance-themed escape room... and each other's arms. (Grumpy/Sunshine, Forced Proximity)

Cuffed by Cupid – A very serious detective. A reckless bartender. One pair of handcuffs and a very inconvenient attraction. (Only One Bed, Enemies-to-Lovers)

Cornered by Cupid – Old flames. New lies. And a fake-couple retreat that forces them to confront the past they never got over. (Second Chance, Fake Dating)

Caught by Cupid – The matchmaker finally meets her match... and she's a smug, gorgeous rival with a smile that spells trouble. (Business Rivals, Enemies-to-Lovers)

Smart banter, swoony tension, and a town full of meddling lesbians. Fall in love four times over in this spicy small-town series where the only thing more unpredictable than love... is who Cupid will target next.

About the Author

CLAERIE HAS SPENT MOST of her life telling stories. She was captivated by the written word at the age of seven when she read her first Magic Tree House book and has ventured to countless far-off places since. She loves to travel and explore new cultures. When she's not writing or dreaming of new book ideas, you can usually find her helping other authors polish their works as a freelance editor—and singing while doing so. Broadway musicals are her soul food, something her mother and sister know well. She constantly blasts the newest soundtrack through the halls of their Missouri home, much to the chagrin of her sassy and spoiled cat.